AUTUMN'S LEGACY

A SEASONS OF MAGIC URBAN FANTASY NOVEL

SARAH BIGLOW

 Formatted with Vellum

SPECIAL THANKS

This edition was made possible by the support of so many wonderful backers on Kickstarter.

But I wanted to say a special thank you to **Myrdd, Clair John, Bill Lisse, Joe G., Jay A. Reynolds, Beth Wrege, Gerald P. McDaniel, Kandi, Lav, Kaitlyn, Cynthia Coffman, Kevin S. Varner, Jeffrey Tristan Thyme, Deborah Hedges, Stacy Shuda, Ryan Scott James, Mothy, Meredith, Seamus Sands and Tommy** for helping the campaign and these books soar higher than I ever imagined possible.

SEPTEMBER 17, 2017

ONE

Giving the place I'd called home for the last six years one last look, I climbed behind the driver seat of the rental truck. I pulled up Kelton and swung a right onto Commonwealth Avenue, well on the way to the next chapter of my life. One where J.T. waited for me at night—or at least on the days he wasn't pulling double shifts.

"I'm proud of you," Dad said from the passenger seat.

I glanced at him as I eased to a stop at a red light. I'd spent a good part of the last decade hating the man beside me. Mostly because of not under-standing what he'd lost and sacrificed the night my mother died. Being forced to save the world and rejoin the magical community had changed my perspective and we were in a better place. One that involved him helping pack up boxes right beside me and moving them to the two-bedroom condo J.T. and I were now renting. I'd spent so much time at his place these last few months, it just made sense to share a lease.

"It was time to move, anyway," I said and pressed on the gas.

He shook his head, a small smile flickering across his lips. "You know, I always liked J.T. I wasn't always in on all the magic stuff when you were growing up, but I remember when you two first met." His smile grew bigger. "You were maybe ten or eleven and you marched right up to him introducing yourself. Not as Ezri, but as the Savior. And he said, "I'm the Healer." It was beautiful."

"I remember that too," I said, smiling to myself.

"Anyway," he continued. "I'm glad you found your way back to each other. And I feel like I haven't said it enough lately, but I'm so glad you're back in my life, Ez."

"I am, too, Dad. And I'm sorry for shutting you out for so long. I was a stubborn kid who thought she knew what was best and what had actually happened when I had no clue. I didn't listen when you tried to tell me ... I was wrong."

"I know your mother would be proud of the woman you've become, too," he said, his expression going misty-eyed.

I know she is. I hadn't gotten up the nerve to tell him that six months ago, I'd communed with her spirit. Or at least a part of her magic she'd left behind for me. I also didn't have the heart to tell him she was gone for good now, sacrificing herself a second time to save me and help stop the Order of Samael's first major attack on my city.

The rest of the trip to the new apartment was quiet, but comfortable. We'd settled farther from the city which meant a longer commute for the both of us. Although it also put us closer to Authority headquarters, a place I'd been spending more and more time at over the summer. It had taken a long time to convince people that they and their children were safe. The fact that only three months ago, a Whisperer named Lola Cox had easily snatched three girls in plain sight was not something that would fade quickly from the collective consciousness. Even though no other children had been taken the adults in the community weren't convinced until I made my presence felt as often as I possibly could. I'd had a healthy hatred for the Order long before they decided abducting children was a good idea, but they'd turned into the Boogeyman for the magical community, looming around every corner.

I'd chosen not to live in fear. I knew another fight was coming my way thanks to one of those little girls having a vision of the future. Her words haunted my dreams at night, not letting me forget that the world was once again asking more of me as its Savior. *When Darkness reaches its height, and Death's child reigns, the last of Harrow's blood must flow forever more or the life blood of the world will be no more.* Thankfully that time hadn't come yet, and I could still prepare.

I pulled into one of the two designated parking spaces for our unit and cut the engine. J.T. stood waiting by the front door of the building in a navy-blue t-shirt and dark black jeans. I honked the horn once and climbed out. He rushed forward, wrapping me into a tight hug and kissed my cheek. "I hid your Order conspiracy board so it doesn't freak your dad out," he whispered in my ear.

"Thanks. And it's not a conspiracy," I laughed.

"Mr. Trenton, good to see you," J.T. said, directing his attention to my dad.

"Been a long time, son. Now, I don't have to remind you to take care of my daughter, do I?"

"No, sir. Besides, Ezri's pretty good at taking care of herself."

"I'll just help with these last few boxes and let the two of you settle in," he said and rounded the back of the truck.

"Dad, aren't you staying for lunch?" I called out just as my phone buzzed in my pocket with an incoming call from my cousin, Desmond. I was silently grateful he didn't know my ringtone for him was "Call Me Maybe."

"I like take-out as much as the next person, but I've got plans," Dad replied with a smirk.

I let the implied jab at my cooking skills slide and answered the call. "Hey Des, please tell me the world isn't ending."

"Not since last I checked. How'd the move go?"

"Still in progress. Dad is helping," I watched as Dad struggled with the hand cart, boxes tipping precariously to one side. "Well, he's trying anyways."

"I heard that," Dad said and disappeared inside with the cart. J.T. followed after him, leaving me alone.

"So, what's up?" I prompted, leaning against the hood of the truck.

"Can't a guy just check in on his cousin to make sure everything went okay with her first move in half a decade?" I could tell by the way his voice slowly inched up from a baritone to a tenor that he was stalling.

"Not when it's you. What's going on?"

"I saw the girls this morning. They're doing better, but Neveah asked me if you'd figured out the prophecy's meaning."

"I'm glad they're healing. And no, no closer to figuring it out. I've poured over my mother's books and even the Authority's journals, but so far nothing jumps out at me. Maybe you can help me look through the records in the library after today's meeting?"

"Sure." The long pause signaled that whatever else he had to tell me wasn't something he really wanted to share. I was intimately familiar with those kinds of silences. They'd punctuated our first reunion in his office when I'd been forced to be cleared by him—the police department psychologist —to return to duty.

"Look, I can tell something's on your mind and I can also tell you don't want to share it. So, I'll just see you later, okay? I need to go make sure Dad and J.T. don't decide to organize."

"See you later." Desmond ended the call, leaving me to traipse up to the second floor with a pit in my stomach. The last time he'd withheld crucial information from me, he'd kept a videotape from my mother hidden away for a decade. Effectively letting me stew in my teenage angst when it all could have been avoided.

It may be hypocritical, but I hated not knowing what was going on with Desmond. He'd put so much pressure on himself to work with Gabby Freeman, Carly Ramirez, and Nevaeh DeWitt, helping them conquer the trauma they'd endured at the hands of the Order. He swore he wasn't putting too much stress on himself, but I didn't believe him. I'd seen the price he paid for using his magic to dig into their memories. So many sleepless nights and how pale it had made him. I worried if he went too far, that he might break. Magic has a way of backfiring on the user when it's overused. Just ask Lola Cox or Kayla.

Their magic had literally turned them invisible, making them Whisperers.

"Oh, I'll take care of those," J.T.'s voice carried from inside the apartment.

"I can handle hanging up some clothes ..." Dad's voice trailed off and I swallowed the lump in my throat as I walked into the bedroom.

Shit. Dad found what J.T. had dubbed my conspiracy board. "You weren't supposed to see that." I rushed forward, pulling the closet door closed.

"And what is it exactly?"

My default was to keep him in the dark about magic. However, he'd known the truth about our family's secret long before I came along. He deserved to know exactly what I'd faced and what Mom had been sacrificed for. I opened the door again, pulled the poster board out, and laid it on the bed we'd already set up.

"This has everything on it that I know about the Order. From when the Authority first recorded their existence to every time that I've crossed paths with them and all the players that I'm aware of." The image of Jamison Taggart sent chills down my spine. "The more I know about their operation, the better prepared I'll be to face this new prophecy."

Neveah's words echoed in my mind again: *'When Darkness reaches its height, and Death's child reigns, the last of Harrow's blood must flow forever more or the life blood of the world will be no more.'*

"How can I help?" Dad crossed his arms over his chest—it must be an inherited trait, because I could swear it was me—and jutted his chin out defiantly.

"I appreciate the offer, Dad. I really do, but it's a magical problem," I set the board back in the closet and scooped up clothes hangers, setting them inside so they obscured the board.

"I know you want to do things on your own, sweetheart, but I'm here for you. I want to help. If it means protecting my daughter, I'll do whatever it takes."

"It can't hurt to get fresh eyes on what you've already looked at. Maybe a non-magical perspective will catch something we missed?" J.T. said, fixing me with a look that clearly said, 'let him in.'

"Yeah, okay. I guess that can't hurt. But I'll have to dig them out of boxes." I knew exactly what boxes contained my mother's pilfered magical texts. Yet, I wanted to keep my dad out of the magical shitstorm that was surely on its way for as long as I could.

"How about this? I'll swing by in the morning, after you've had a chance to unpack a little. I'll see what I can find then," Dad offered.

"Sure. That works." I wrapped him in a hug, and he kissed the top of my head, like he'd done a million times since I was a kid. "I love you."

"I love you, too, Ez."

I DIDN'T WAIT for J.T. to turn off the car before I jumped out of the passenger seat and raced inside, up the staircase to the meeting room. Instinct told me Desmond would be waiting for me. I found him standing by the far windows, staring out at the scenery beyond. Avery, his girlfriend and my favorite tech whiz, stood beside him. She turned first and gave me a smile.

"Hey, Ezri," she said.

"Hi." I focused in on Desmond. "What couldn't you tell me over the phone?"

Avery nudged Desmond in the side, and he gave an audible exhale before he turned around, a broad grin on his face. "Don't be mad," he began, closing the distance between us. "But we didn't want to make a huge deal out of it."

"A huge deal of what?" I demanded, my gaze shifting between the two of them.

Desmond reached out and took Avery's hand. My eyes followed the gesture, noticing a slim silver band on my cousin's ring finger. "Shut up."

"Surprise!" Avery beamed, holding out her left hand to show off a matching band. "We went down to City Hall this morning."

"Why didn't you tell me you were getting married, you jerk?" I pulled him into a bear hug.

"Like I said, we didn't want to make it a huge deal," he repeated.

I turned to eye Avery. "You didn't want the whole church and reception?"

"Nah. Religion's not really my thing. Besides we'll have a party later to celebrate." She leaned in. "I told him we should have you and J.T. as witnesses, but he insisted we keep it quiet."

"What are we keeping quiet?" J.T. appeared in the doorway behind us.

"Desmond got married without me," I answered before Desmond could speak.

"You know she's going to hold that against you for the rest of your life," J.T. laughed, but offered his hand to Desmond.

"Worth it," he replied.

I stepped to the side and Avery followed me. "He was really worried that you were going to be mad," she whispered.

"I've never seen him as happy as when he's with you. I'm thrilled." Avery twisted the band on her finger. "Is there another reason you didn't want a big wedding?" I gestured toward her stomach.

"Oh, no. Maybe one day, but no, not now."

I mimed wiping sweat off my brow and she laughed. "I mean, it's awesome either way obviously."

"It feels good to be part of the family," Avery said just as the doors to the meeting room opened.

Belladonna Montes appeared; the color drained from her usually dark complexion. I hadn't seen much of her since her son, Adrian, died three months ago in an explosion. The same incident had claimed three law enforcement officers too. Part of me still felt responsible for not bringing her son home alive.

"You need to come quickly," she said, her eyes wide as she addressed me. "Something's happened. Yvette Covington's lost her magic."

So much for the world not ending.

TWO

We followed Belladonna back down to the first floor. Instead of making the turn to the library like I expected, she led us back to the kitchen. Memories of our first meeting flashed through my thoughts—the kind way she'd spoken and the overeager interest her son had expressed. We still weren't entirely sure he'd been a willing participant in the kidnappings three months ago, but I'd clearly missed something upon meeting Adrian. A regret I'd have to live with for the rest of my life. I left my entourage in the hallway.

Yvette Covington sat on the bench, resting her head in her hands as a young boy clung to her side. His big brown eyes tracked every movement around him. As I approached, he burrowed further into his mother's protective embrace. Yvette was relatively new to her seat on the Council and I didn't know her well.

"Yvette, what's going on?" I sat across from her on the other side of the table.

"It's gone," she whispered, not meeting my gaze.

"That's not possible," I stated.

Her gaze shot up to meet mine. "I can't feel it anymore. I even tried to do a simple spell, and nothing happened. I feel empty, like a piece of me is missing."

"Let's not panic. I'm sure there's an explanation for what's going on," I said and tried to give her a calming look. "How long ago did you try to do the spell?"

"Right after I got here."

"Okay." If she'd done magic that recently, I should be able to pick up traces of it without trying too hard. "I'm going to try something, but in order to know if it works, I need to know what your magic smells like."

"Eucalyptus."

I nodded and reached beneath my shirt to find the pentacle pendant and sandalwood charm I always wore. I inhaled deeply, letting the charm wash my senses clean. Every time this ritual came with a little tingle at the back of my nose, preparing me to take in the world anew.

I blew out the breath and let the space tell me about all the magic that had been used recently. I picked up on a hint of strawberry from my own magic putting my intent out into the world and a vague taste of spearmint. Desmond must have done some magic recently, too. No sign of eucalyptus anywhere.

"I'm not picking up anything, but that doesn't mean your magic's gone. Like you said, the spell didn't work. So that could explain why I'm not picking it up." I opened my eyes to find Yvette's dark grey gaze boring into me. Her short blonde bob framed her face, highlighting the paleness to her skin.

"I'm telling you that I can't feel it anymore."

"Mommy, I'm scared," the boy said from beside her.

I turned my attention to the child. "What's your name?" In the six months since I'd been back on the Council, I'd never met her son. Actually, we didn't talk much about anything other than Council business.

"Alex," he answered.

"I know this seems scary, Alex, but you're being really brave for your mom."

"It went away," he said.

"What did?"

"The world," he answered.

I looked back to Yvette. "Has he already come into his magic? He's pretty young."

"Not that I sensed," Yvette responded.

"Alex, can you make things happen if you think really hard?" I probed.

He nodded, but then shook his head. "I try and it went away with Mommy's."

"I'll be right back." I retreated to the hall where J.T. and Desmond waited. Belladonna and Avery were nowhere to be seen. "How much do you know about the connection between parents and their children's magic?"

"Nothing. Why, did she really lose her magic?" J.T. replied.

"I don't know. She claims to have tried to cast a spell when she got here, but it didn't work. I didn't pick up on her magic just now either. Yet if the spell didn't work, then I would expect it not to show up." I rubbed at my chin. "But her son, who seems awfully young to have come into his powers, says he can't feel his either. That it disappeared at the same time his mother's did."

"Well, I mean magic is passed through the maternal bloodline. That much we do know. So, if something happened to his mother's abilities, theoretically it could affect his, too," Desmond chimed in.

"I've just never seen it manifest in a kid as young as Alex. I mean, I knew about magic, but I couldn't really do much with it until I was at least eight or nine. He can't be more than five."

"Every child is different," Desmond answered

and for a second the haunted look he'd had right after we'd rescued Neveah surfaced.

"I'm going to see what else I can get out of Yvette. I mean, if we can figure out where she was or what she was doing when it happened, that will make it easier to undo whatever it is."

"Be careful," J.T. and Desmond said in unison.

"Guys, relax, I'm just going to ask her questions." I waved away their concern that I was about to do something foolish and returned to Yvette in the kitchen.

"I'm going to help you in whatever way I can. You have my word on that. But I need to know more about what you were doing when it happened. Where you were ... Everything you can tell me." I sat back down across from her.

Yvette scrunched up her face and shook her head. "It's hazy, kind of like I know it's there but I can't remember."

I looked at Alex. "Do you remember where you and your mom were before you came here, and the world went away?"

The boy shook his head. "It's empty."

"Okay. I have an idea of how to see what you did. It's risky, but it works."

"Have you done it before?"

Yes, except the last time was on a dying woman in a coma. "Plenty of times."

She nodded for me to go ahead. I could see Desmond and J.T. lingering just out of view in the hallway. Somehow they had known what I was about to do before I did. Time to throw caution to the wind.

THREE

I focused on Yvette's face, reached across the table and took her hands in mine. The more points of contact, the better chance I had of connecting. Her hands trembled against mine and I squeezed them in reassurance. Alex still sat beside his mother, watching me work with eyes wide.

"All you need to do is breathe and focus on the last thing you do remember from today before everything went weird," I instructed.

"I'll try," she whispered. After a beat she added, "I remember being at home. We were going out somewhere."

"Good. Just hold onto that memory."

"What are you going to do?" The tinge of nerves made her voice jump an octave.

"I'm just going to come along for the ride. Now, remember to breathe."

She gave several audible inhales and exhales. I took in air through my nose and expelled it through my mouth, letting the world start to fall away. The scent of fresh fruit bloomed around me, wrapping around our joined hands, securing the bond between us. I could feel my own magic calling to hers, seeking a boost, but nothing happened. Maybe she was right, and something had suppressed her magic. I pushed that question aside and turned my focus to following her memory.

I eased into Yvette's memory. Alex sat at a small kitchen island kicking his feet against the chair on which he sat. Yvette stood by the stove, a look of panic on her face as she tried to salvage burned French toast.

"Mommy, I'm hungry," Alex whined.

"I know, sweetie."

"I want Daddy to make breakfast."

"Daddy isn't home right now." Yvette set the spatula and burnt remnants aside. "But, how about as a special treat you and Mommy go out to breakfast, just the two of us."

"Can we?" He hopped off the chair, a broad smile on his face.

"Go put on your shoes."

Alex raced from the room. Yvette turned off the stove and grabbed her car keys. The next moment they were sitting in a restaurant that bustled with patrons. A thick stack of pre-cut French toast sat on a plate in front of Alex.

"Thanks Mommy," he said before digging in.

I put a little distance between myself and the memory, trying to take in the surroundings, reaching out with my magical senses for anything that didn't belong. It was a skill I'd been developing since the summer, especially with memory manipulation being a go to trick for the Order. The diner wasn't one I recognized, even so that didn't mean much. There were a million little diners all around the state. I took in the other patrons, the people that Yvette hadn't taken notice of. Some of them had blurred faces, a condition I tried to mitigate with a little exertion of my own power. I only succeeded in giving the people generic eyes, noses and mouths. Useful characteristics remained unintelligible.

"Come on, show me something," I muttered to the memory space around me.

The memory around me sharpened, as if my words had weight. Yvette and Alex dimmed, and I spotted a thin shimmer from Yvette's head, racing back along the booths to another patron. I leaned forward, touching the shimmer to find it was as real as I was. It twanged like a guitar string under my touch.

"What is this?" My question didn't yield any answers, so I followed the trail around the corner booth to a man sitting there with a cup of coffee in his hand. The feeling around me changed. Whatever I was seeing was not a part of Yvette's memory. The man's gaze remained locked on Yvette and Alex. I

studied the table in front of him, taking note of the unused utensils and the twenty already sitting beneath the sugar container. Whoever he was, he didn't intend to be bothered. I moved to the empty booth seat directly behind him and peered over his shoulder. It was then that I noticed the placemat beneath his left hand was at an angle.

"What are you hiding?" I tugged the placemat away to find a slender envelope with Yvette's name and the number 1 scrawled on it in thick marker.

Setting the placemat back on the table, I stepped back, intending to assess the shimmer connecting the man to Yvette when the man's head turned, and his dark olive gaze met my own. "You aren't supposed to be here," he hissed.

"I get that a lot."

The shimmer intensified despite the fact the man wasn't engaging with Yvette anymore. A familiar scent accosted my nose, sending me staggering back a step. Vinegar. It tickled a different memory. One I'd pieced together from Gabby's mind three months ago. I'd pegged it as garlic then, but it could have been Taggart's magic within me playing tricks. In my gut, I had no doubt this was magic from the bastard who had tortured Carly and Gabby. Trying to see if they had the gift of premonition. My hands balled into fists, and I prepared to take a swing when the world around me suddenly vanished.

"What the ..." I trailed off before a few choice words could escape and give Alex a new vocabulary.

"Did you find out what happened?" Yvette looked worn out, with dark circles forming beneath her eyes. Alex curled farther into his mother's torso.

"Sort of. Everything was going along and then it just disappeared."

"I told you it's gone," Yvette moaned.

"I'm going to find a way to fix this." I had more information than I did ten minutes ago. I still wanted to dissect that shimmer. Nevertheless, experience told me with Yvette in this condition, she wasn't in a headspace to let me go digging deeper through her memory. "For now, why don't you go home and rest. I'll bring the rest of the Council up to speed."

"How can it just be gone?" Yvette whispered, clutching her son close.

That was the question I intended to answer. Just because my closest allies hadn't heard of it, didn't mean it hadn't happened in the past. Clearly someone had figured out a way to achieve this result. I wasn't convinced it meant her magic was wholly gone either. Besides, the way magic had always been taught to me was that it existed in the world like a natural force similar to gravity or inertia. It existed inside us, too and could never be truly destroyed. It's why I carried Taggart's stone spell inside of me. I was strong enough to keep it from turning me into a statue, but it had to go somewhere months ago. It couldn't just disappear. Meaning if I could find the asshole from the diner, I could find Yvette and Alex's magic.

WALKING BACK into the meeting room set my nerves on edge. The semi-circle of chairs had been assembled and eleven of the thirteen seats were filled. The door closed behind me and all eyes landed on me.

"So, uh, I'm not sure how many people know yet, but it seems that someone has taken Yvette Covington's magic and her son's abilities along with it," I stated it as matter-of-factly as possible before taking my spot beside Desmond.

"What do you mean taken?" Richard Henley, a balding man in his fifties, demanded.

"From what I could tell by going through her memory, someone siphoned it off. She can't feel her power anymore and she doesn't remember the attack," I answered.

"Magic is part of a person's make-up, just like blood or DNA. It can't be gone," Belladonna insisted.

"I understand that. I don't have a better explanation right now. But what I can tell you is I'm going to figure out what's going on and why, and stop it from happening again.'

J.T. leaned close and whispered in my ear, "Please tell me the Order isn't rearing its ugly head again.'

"Looks like it. Sorry."

"Damn."

I waited for more questions, but none came. Either everyone had the same questions as Richard and Belladonna, or they were too scared to probe more. I opened my mouth to share what I'd seen under the placemat, but decided against it. It was more likely to incite panic. Although I didn't know enough to pass this information along and keep it contained.

"We should continue with today's meeting and I'll check in with Yvette later," I said, hoping to move our focus to the reason we'd called this meeting.

A small group had been putting together a proposal for increased education and cross-training specifically for kids who were coming into their abilities. After what had happened to the girls back in June, we needed to be proactive. They might not be able to tap into their abilities by age seven or eight, but they needed to know how their skills worked, and what it looked like when magic happened to and around them.

"We're all agreed that general classes need to begin with the elementary-school aged children," Richard said. "But, putting a lot of it on the families is onerous."

"People in other communities have managed to pass down their gifts generation to generation just through families without a problem," I countered, watching Belladonna flinch at my words.

I hadn't expected her to back my proposal that families should take a more active role in teaching their children about magic, but she'd been the first to sign on to the suggestion. Maybe it was guilt that her decisions had deprived her son of learning about all of his heritage. Or possibly she truly believed that it was the responsibility of a parent to guide and protect their child. Either way, I was glad to have her on my side.

"But, we're not a part of those communities," Richard retorted.

"Careful Rich, your privilege is showing," Desmond said just loud enough to make the other man flush.

"I don't think it would be that hard," Laurie McGinn said from the other end of the semi-circle. "We could develop a standard curriculum that all families would use as a starting point. Sure, some instruction would vary depending on the family and their magic abilities, but we can put that together." When Richard gave her a raised brow, she fixed him with a knowing smile. "I'm a public-school teacher, remember? I volunteer to spearhead setting this up. You wouldn't have to do a thing, Rich."

"Fine. Bring it to the next meeting and if it gets a

majority vote, we'll move it along." He looked around the room. "Any other business we need to discuss?"

I raised a hand and all eyes fell on me again. "Not business exactly, but I think we should all take a minute to congratulate our very own Desmond for leaving the bachelor life behind."

Desmond shot me an annoyed look. Despite that he grinned as people stood, clapped him on the back, and offered him handshakes. I leaned back in my chair and let my cousin bask in the happiness. He'd hid the actual ceremony from me. He could live with me embarrassing him for a little while.

"How worried should we be about what happened to Yvette?" J.T. asked, lacing his fingers through mine.

"It's a problem. When Des is done riding the congratulations wave, I'll fill you both in."

"Is it something the rest of the group should know?" He prodded.

"I don't know what it means yet. No need to make them panic if I don't have all the facts. Just trust me, okay?"

Desmond extricated himself from the group to join J.T. and I. "So, can we talk for a minute?"

He marched off toward the tech space before either J.T. or I could respond. So, we followed after him in silence. He eased the door shut. I expected Avery to be waiting for us, but she was gone.

"I know when you're not saying things, Ez. It's kind of my job, remember? So, spill it."

I hated that he knew me so well, even though we'd only been back in each other's lives a short time. "I saw something in Yvette's memory. The guy who took her magic, he had an envelope with her name and the number one written on it. I didn't see what was inside, but I'm guessing it had pictures or something, so he knew who to target."

"Number one typically means there's more to follow," Desmond said, the joy melting from his features.

"I know. But I haven't figured out where that information came from or how he even managed to take her magic."

J.T. reached down and squeezed my hand. "Why do I get the feeling this means another trip into Yvette's memory, but in your own head?"

I flashed him a small smile. "Because you know me so well."

"You're not doing it alone. You throw yourself into danger too easily, Ez. Besides, it's reckless," Desmond added.

"Des, I'm the Savior. It means I go first into this fight."

"We both love you, but you aren't indestructible. Or did you forget you've almost turned to stone twice now?" Des scowled at me, clearly unnerved by the memory.

"I haven't forgotten." I reflexively touched the left side of my rib cage. "I carry that possibility with me every day. Even so if I'm afraid of it, that gives the bad guys power. I refuse to cede anything to those murderous assholes." I reached out with my left hand and took Desmond's so that I held both their hands. "Look, I'm not going to be alone in this. I've got both of you backing me up."

J.T. turned to Desmond. "I'm not going to let anything happen to her. You have my word."

"The minute you find out anything, you need to call me," Desmond replied. "They're worried out there as it is. The more information we can give them, the better."

"I'm on it." I gave his hand one last squeeze before he left the room.

"You can bring people into memories with you, right?" J.T. asked as we followed in Desmond's wake.

"I'll need you on the outside, monitoring me," I said, not answering his question directly.

"You've been physically attacked doing this more times than I'd like. I'm going in as back-up."

I huffed in annoyance. "Fine ... But we better get to it. Desmond's not wrong about everyone being on edge. The sooner I can solve this, the better." Now I just had to hope my own memory of what I'd seen was enough to provide the answers.

FOUR

Settling on the couch—our only piece of living room furniture assembled at the moment—I cleansed my magical palette again. The cushions shifted as J.T. sat beside me, taking my right hand in his left.

"So, how do we do this?"

"You try not to do anything magical. I've signal boosted Des before. However, the last time I went into my own memory, I had a non-magical person along for the ride."

"Got it. Keep my sweet powers in check."

God his puns were terrible and I love them. "You should be able to move around inside as an observer," I added.

Concentrating, I let my own magic build up around us, wrapping tight around our joined hands and pulling the memory to the forefront of my brain.

With a single exhale we slipped into the memory. I watched myself watching Yvette with Alex, and the Order member.

"This is wild," J.T. said from beside me.

"Yeah. Look, I need to examine that shimmer. See what else you can find out from the envelope under that guy's placemat," I directed.

"You mean the guy you just approached?"

I looked to find Memory Me examining the man. "Give me a second," I told J.T. and poured out a little extra power, willing the memory to pause. "Okay, try it now."

The mental pause button thrummed at the base of my skull, reminding me that even I have limits in a memory of my own making. So, I closed in on the booth where Yvette and Alex sat to get a close-up look at the shimmer connecting her to the man across the room. Upon closer inspection, it looked like single strands of hair or fiber. I ran my fingertips along the top and bottom of it, expecting it to be wispy and vaporous, but it was a solid mass connecting the two.

It was only my memory of someone else's altered thoughts, but if I could figure out how to reverse it here, I could duplicate it in the real world. So, I poured out even more will, strawberry permeating everything around me, trying to get the siphoned magic to reverse course and return home. Instead, everything around us began to shake, the memory-within-a-memory starting to break down.

"We need to go," I called to J.T.

"I've almost got it," he said, holding up the folder.

The space around me tilted on its axis and my stomach sloshed. "Leave it here. I don't think we can take it with us. And we really need to go. *Now.*"

J.T. tipped the envelope on its side, letting the contents spill into his hand. I couldn't see what he'd found, but my vision began going blurry at the same time. My head pounded as the memory resumed playing out. The man's head swiveled to look at Memory Me. At the same time I reached out and pulled J.T. with me, back to the safety of our condo.

The space spun in dizzying circles around me and I hung my head between my knees to keep the nausea at bay. J.T.'s hand pressed into the small of my back, rubbing concentric circles.

"Told you that you needed back-up," he said before the couch cushion shifted beside me and his hand fell away.

"Heal now, please ... lecture later," I moaned as he handed me a glass of water and some aspirin. Not what I'd hoped for, but I couldn't expect my healer boyfriend to use his own powers every time I had a headache. Magic comes with a price, even if it's a small one.

So, I downed the pills and drained the glass, tasting a hint of honey in the aftertaste. Maybe he'd given them a boost after all, because the pain in my head subsided faster than normal.

"So, what did you find?" I asked, sitting up and leaning against the back of the couch. I closed my eyes to ensure the world didn't continue to spin.

"It looked like city records of Yvette's house. How long she's owned it, property taxes and things like that. There was also a list of names scrawled on the back ..."

The way he trailed off told me there was more to what he'd found. I opened my eyes and looked at him. "Whose names?"

He rubbed at his chin, not meeting my gaze. "Ours. The whole council."

A lump formed in my throat, making it hard to breathe. The Order had found out who was on the council. I shouldn't have been surprised. It's been primarily hereditary since its founding and I knew of at least one high-ranking Order member who'd started out on our side of the fight. Before he was a sleazeball FBI Agent hell-bent on orchestrating ritual murders, Jamison Taggart was just another Authority member. "Shit."

"It definitely doesn't look good. What about you? Could you figure out the spell?" J.T.'s words washed over me, pushing thoughts of Taggart away.

"No." I propped my elbows on my knees, gesturing with my hands. "In the memory, at least, it felt solid, like a cable connecting two machines. I tried to reverse the flow and that's when everything started to destabilize."

"It was a memory though, you couldn't change what happened," J.T. commented, sitting back down beside me.

"I just thought if I could figure it out there, I could do it here. Maybe give Yvette and her son back what was taken."

"And you pushed yourself too much in the process. Even you, oh great Savior, have limits."

"I'm aware of that. But that title also comes with responsibility that only I can bear," I reminded him.

He cupped my cheek in his hand. "I love you, but you take too much on yourself. We are finally in a good place, better than we've ever been. Despite that, I can't shake this feeling that if you keep going like this, pushing boundaries, chasing down the bad guys, I'm going to lose you." He pressed his thumb to my lips to keep any retort quiet. "It's not because you're a cop. I'm scared that witch Ezri is going to bite off more than she can chew."

I kissed the pad of his thumb and leaned against his shoulder. "Not going to happen. Not when I have you and Desmond supporting me. And I know that I can call on the Council for help if I ever really needed it."

"You're going to tell them what we found, aren't' you?"

"Yes. Of course, I am." I pursed my lips as the

weight of Taggart's spell pressed against my ribs. I didn't want to pay that bastard another visit. It wouldn't be useful since he'd deny any knowledge of what's going on. Besides, if he'd passed on the names of the Council, he'd have done it when he switched sides. Not now. Which posed the question: *Why now?*

"You got lost for a minute," J.T. whispered.

I snuggled deeper into his embrace. "Sorry, just thinking about whether or not it's worth it to see Taggart."

"I'm off shift tomorrow. If you do decide to pay that creep a visit, I'll go with you. I don't like the idea of you being alone with him."

"He's shackled, J.T. And the last time I saw him, I beat his ass magically-speaking. He doesn't scare me. I just have a feeling he wouldn't tell me the truth, even if he knew what was happening."

"Your dad's coming over tomorrow right? Maybe he can dig into records and see if anyone else changed sides."

"It does seem pretty safe, sticking Dad on research duty." After all, he wasn't magical so he shouldn't be in the Order's crosshairs.

J.T. fell silent beside me and I let the peaceful-ness of our new home wash over me. Sure, there were boxes to be unpacked and art to hang, but it still felt like home.

"So, you really didn't know anything about Des and Avery?" His question broke the silence.

"Not a thing. I can't believe he didn't even want me there. So much for him being all about family," I grumbled.

"I know. It did seem a little out of character for him to make such a big decision without the rest of his inner circle being involved." J.T. leaned forward. "Do you think it's a baby?"

"Avery said no. I didn't ask in so many words, but it was heavily implied and she shot it down."

"What about you?"

"Uh, last I checked we were using protection," I said, unintentionally putting distance between us.

"I meant marriage. What do you think about the idea of marriage?"

"I love you but ... we're still young, J.T. We just found our way back to each other. I don't want to rush into something."

His face fell and I knew it wasn't the answer he'd been expecting. "I'm not saying never. Just not right now. Besides, you know Des would say we were just copying him." Images of J.T. trying to dress and act like a preteen Desmond flashed through my brain. Back before I'd pushed everyone I loved and who loved me away.

J.T. nodded and smiled. Though it was tight-lipped. "You're right. I was just joking."

"No, you weren't," I said, brushing strands of

hair out of his eyes. "And I love you all the more for it. Now, I need to check in at work. I'll be back in an hour or two. Don't eat all the takeout without me."

"Wouldn't dream of it."

I left him sitting on the couch, no doubt trying to piece together how that conversation could have gone a million different ways. He wasn't the only one. I hadn't dated seriously since high school. I'd had a good example of a solid relationship from childhood with my parents. Even so, like everything else in my life, my mother's death cast a dark shadow over wanting to let anyone in. Before her death, I would have swooned at just the thought of marrying J.T. and would have jumped on board with it at the drop of a hat. That wasn't me anymore. Neither of us were who we were back then.

FIVE

The precinct was slow when I arrived forty minutes later. I gave a nod to the desk sergeant and headed for my desk in the bullpen. Jacquie, my partner, sat at her desk, pouring over a case file.

"Hey," I said, nudging the back of her chair as I passed.

She looked up. "Thought you weren't coming in today."

"Got done with things early so figured I'd check in. I miss anything important?"

"Nope." She glanced around the space and then nodded for me to follow her.

I ignored the unease creeping up my spine as I followed her into a vacant witness interview room. "Please tell me you've figured something out about this damn prophecy," she whispered.

"I've been trying to decipher it all summer. The most I can figure out is whatever the Order has up their sleeve, is happening at or near the Winter Solstice ... and I have to stop them. Yet again. But the whole Death's child thing, not a clue."

"Denise says that Neveah isn't sleeping. She just keeps going on about it. Like it won't leave her be."

"Desmond mentioned she was doing better in their sessions."

Jacquie crossed her arms over her chest and hung her head. "I think she puts on a brave face for him and the other girls. She wants her friends to heal and be okay, but she's putting her own trauma on the back burner."

I leaned against the closed door behind me. "Do you know if Desmond has gone through her memories with her to try and parse what she went through?"

Jacquie shook her head. "She doesn't talk about it with me. She knows you're my partner and that you rescued her. Even so I think she's realizing that I can't protect her from magic."

"Jacquie, I'm sorry. It has to be hard being on the outside, but knowing everything you do," I said.

"Don't worry about my feelings, Ezri. I get it. But I think she'll feel better and be able to move forward once she knows that you've gotten it sorted out. That you know what's coming and you're ready."

"I'm working as fast as I can, but prophecies are

kind of vague by nature. And with everything else that's just dropped in my lap ..."

"What's happened now?"

Now was as good a time as any to fill her in. I let out a slow breath. "One of the Council members, Yvette Covington, had her magic stolen. And it's affecting her son, too. It looks like it was a targeted Order attack and if I'm right, she's only the beginning. I think there was a list. They could be coming after all of us."

"How do you know it's them?" Her words said they didn't believe me. Whereas the way her face paled and her gaze narrowed, said she believed me.

"I went into her memory and I saw the man who was taking her magic. I could smell his magic." I paused and swallowed. "It was the same man who tortured the girls."

My partner's gaze turned steely, making her usually dark brown irises look metallic. "I'm in."

I appreciated her unwavering support, but this wasn't a case for the police. "I'm not sure what you can do on this one. There's no crime we can investigate. Yvette doesn't even remember what happened. And it's not like we can say she was drugged, because we both know that's not the Order's M.O."

"Whoever this bastard is, he hurt my niece. I want his balls in a vice."

"Believe me, I want him to hurt just as much as

the girls did. We don't have any concrete evidence to get you involved officially."

"Unless Neveah or Carly identify him." Jacquie offered.

"The cases are closed. Lola Cox admitted to kidnapping them and none of the girls could identify the people holding them. They couldn't even offer up a sketch, remember?"

"Trauma victims recall pieces of memory months later. Ezri, please. Neveah isn't the only one haunted by what happened. If I'd been around ..."

"She'd still have been taken, because Lola was damn good at what she did. She could literally turn invisible and you wouldn't have seen her coming. Whisperers make great low-level flunkies," I cut her off. "If there's anything I need from you on this, I'll call you. I promise."

Jacquie reached out a hand to stop me from leaving the room. "Where'd it happen, this magic theft?'

"A diner. I didn't get a look at the name, or rather, they scrubbed it from Yvette's memory. Why?"

Jacquie shook her head. "I was just thinking about that girl from the Italian restaurant in the North End. The waitress you connected to the Order back in March."

"Kevin Ellery's ex-girlfriend, Gabrielle? Why her?"

"I'm not sure. She was an informant for them before, even if she didn't realize it. Maybe she knows something now." After a beat, she added, "I'm probably just reading into things."

"Not a bad idea, actually. Could you pay her a visit, see what she knows, and maybe swing by the prison? See if Taggart is any more forthcoming with you."

"You think he's still got his fingers in the pie?"

I raked my fingers through my hair. "He used to be on our side. Who knows what other information he took with him? It may have been a decade ago, but the leadership hasn't changed that much. It's still the same families on the council, so they could be working off intel he gave them."

"Even if he had this information, why would he hold onto it until now?" Jacquie posed.

"I've been asking myself the same question all afternoon. They don't do anything without a reason and a plan. Whatever this is, it's important and it probably has something to do with what's coming." I rubbed at my eyes. "I hate feeling like we're always one step behind. They knew there was another prophecy out there before we did. If I'm being honest, if they hadn't taken the girls, we might have never known about what Neveah saw."

"We know now," Jacquie replied. "Go on, you should fill your people in. I'll see what I can dig up on my end and get back to you."

"Don't give up on her Jacquie. Whether she knows it or not, she needs your type of protection just as much as her magic."

"Thanks." Jacquie gestured for me to open the door and together we stepped into the hallway leading back to the bullpen. "I'm going to dig into Taggart's known associates while I'm at it. See if any of them pop up as being possible members of this little cult."

I didn't entirely agree with her assessment of the Order as a cult; mostly because when it came right down to it, our recruiting methods weren't all that different. We approached new magical families offering them guidance, protection, and a place to learn magic. We didn't promise unlimited power like the Order, but it was still a grassroots effort. Like with all things magic, intention was the defining characteristic. Looking at two magical practitioners you wouldn't be able to tell the difference until they actually used their gifts for good or ill.

I started down the hallway, addressing Jacquie's statement as I went. "Good thinking. The more faces we can add to the board of players, the better."

I wasn't looking forward to filling in the Council on what I'd learned. Especially since I knew people would demand answers on how to protect themselves. Honestly, I still had no idea how the Order member had done what he'd done. Jacquie followed me back to the bullpen and I caught sight of Captain

Beech in her office. She glanced up and gave me a small nod before going back to her paperwork.

"Just watch your back," Jacquie warned, clapping me on the shoulder before grabbing her keys and jacket.

I had every intention of being careful. That didn't mean the world was going to be so accommodating. Just as I got back to my car, a message flashed on my screen from Desmond. *'SOS—emergency meeting. Get here now.'*

RAISED voices greeted me as I approached the second-floor meeting room. People hadn't bothered to sit down in their usual seats. Richard sat on the end, looking dazed and pale.

"What's going on?" I demanded of the group, not caring who answered.

"I ... I don't remember," he answered, looking up at me with watery eyes.

I had a guess of what might have happened, given the way Yvette's symptoms—for lack of a better description—presented. Her general confusion and missing memory looked to be much like the same state in which Richard now found himself. "Richard, I need you to tell me what your magic smells like. Can you do that?"

Richard's gaze darted around the room, landing

briefly on each of the other women in the room before settling back on me, his cheeks warming in embarrassment. "Roses."

Not the most masculine of scents, but who was I to judge. "Okay." I put a hand on his shoulder and addressed the rest of the room. "I need everyone to wait outside. Downstairs would be even better and don't use any magic."

"Why not?" Richard asked weakly beside me.

"Because I need to see if you've still got yours."

Desmond and J.T. shepherded everyone else from the room, closing the doors behind them. I let the sandalwood charm wash away the faint hints of J.T.'s soothing magic from my senses before I turned my attention back to Richard.

"Okay, let's see what we're working with." I took a couple steps back and pointed to the chair at the far end of the room. "Move that chair to right below the window." I gestured to the far side of the room.

"I'll try." The bluster and macho attitude were gone as he squinted and held out a hand, like a magician on television. I guess those depictions had to come from somewhere. Beads of perspiration broke out along his hairline and upper lip, but nothing happened. I didn't detect any hint of roses. I also couldn't sense any hint of vinegar, which meant if Richard's magic had been stripped, the man I'd seen in Yvette's memory wasn't the culprit this time.

"Richard, do you remember our meeting this morning?" I felt myself shifting to cop mode.

"Yes. Someone took Yvette's magic."

"That's right. Do you remember where you went once the meeting was done?"

"I ... I went to get something to eat."

"Where? Do you remember who was with you? Have you checked in with your family?"

"I was with my mother. We always go for an early dinner on Sundays."

"What about a wife? Kids?" I pressed.

He shook his head, wiping the sweat from his brow. "Never married. No kids that I know of."

"Do you and your mother go to the same place for dinner every week?" I doubted they would go to a diner that served breakfast all day. Though then again, I hadn't known he was unmarried and had no children.

"Yes. It's her favorite place. It's in the North End."

My heart sank. I didn't know of any diners in the North End like the one I'd seen in Yvette's memory. The fact that they were both attacked in public suggested they were being followed. He'd been in the North End, giving more credence to Jacquie's question about Gabrielle. "Do you remember the name of it?"

Richard pulled out his phone and showed me his GPS with the address of the restaurant. I didn't have a photographic memory or anything, but it sure looked like the same restaurant where Jacquie was heading right now.

"Do me a favor, call your mother and see if her magic's been affected. Then, go home and try to rest. I'm working on a way to fix this." Time to do a little detective work of my own.

Parking near North Station, I traced the cobblestone and brick sidewalks of the North End until I found the tiny restaurant that I'd visited with Jacquie six months ago. It was just like dozens of other places around, using the small space to pack in as many patrons as possible. I had no way of knowing if the woman I needed to see was even working, but it was all I had to go on. I didn't see Jacquie anywhere so I assumed she'd paid Taggart a visit first.

A tiny bell tinkled above my head, announcing my entrance. The place was busy, but not overly crowded. I eyed the dessert display at the front of the restaurant and remembered the last time I'd seen Gabrielle, the ex-girlfriend of an innocent man she'd condemned to be a gargoyle for five years. I'd watched her have what she thought was a private conversation when Jacquie and I had turned up asking questions about her ex, Kevin. I hadn't known at the time Gabrielle had been filling Agent Taggart in on our investigating. Gabrielle hadn't known he'd been using Kevin to murder people.

"Hi, can I help ..." a female voice started from behind me.

I caught her reflection in the glass of the display. So, Gabrielle was working today. I pivoted and gave her a smile. "I hope so."

Gabrielle took a couple steps back. "I'm not talking to you. I haven't broken any laws and the last time you came here, you ruined my life."

"Ruined your life? Really ... Someone you claimed to care about is sitting in prison, because you let bad people use his own gifts against him." I took a breath. "I'd reconsider that decision," I added, following her back through the restaurant, past the noisy kitchen and out the back to a dead-end alley.

"Why are you here?" She shoved her hands into the pockets of her dark jeans.

"Because I need to ask you some questions." I pulled up a picture of Richard. "Have you seen him come in today?"

"I don't know." She didn't even bother to look at the image.

"Helps to actually look at what I'm showing you, Gabrielle."

She shifted her weight in a nervous gesture, but

finally looked at my phone. "Maybe. He looks like a lot of guys who come in. He a suspect or something?"

"Victim ... Of a magical attack and your old buddies are behind it."

"Look, I'm not with them anymore. They used me without my knowledge and I cut ties."

I gestured to the brand on her wrist. "That says otherwise."

"Can anyone who regrets a tattoo get it removed? No. Just because it's still there doesn't mean I'm a part of it anymore."

I sighed. "Gabrielle, I don't know you very well, but I know the Order. They don't just let you walk away. So, tell me what happened to this man? Help me and I'll help get you free of them."

Gabrielle snorted and for a split second I was reminded of the look Lola Cox had given me when I had tried to offer her the same freedom. The look that clearly told me 'the only way you get out from under them is death.' "You may be some savior or whatever, but you can't help me."

"I can't if you won't let me. You're right, they used you to get to Kevin, so they had a fall guy for their messed-up ritual. And he's paying the price for that with prison time. Don't let these people screw you over again. Tell me what you know. I have friends who can protect you."

"What, the police?"

"A little higher up than that," I replied. "Please,

people are losing their magic. I need to know what you know."

She wrung her hands and averted her gaze. "I got told that I was supposed to look out for that guy. They gave me instructions on what to do. I didn't really understand them, but I did what I was told. They said once I delivered the magic, they'd let me go."

"Written instructions?" I probed.

She shook her head. "No, it was more like they put something in my head and it just kind of triggered what I had to do."

Like a sleeper program. Somehow, I doubted Mr. Vinegar had those instructions. He seemed the type to take action on his own rather than have someone else controlling him. The thought crossed my mind of going into Gabrielle's memory, but J.T. was right. I had limits and I couldn't keep bringing other people's trauma into my own mind. I hadn't shared it with him or Desmond, but for weeks after we solved the kidnappings, I'd had recurring dreams about the girls in captivity.

"Do you remember what you did? What the instructions told you to do?"

"No. Look, I did what they asked and I'm sorry you got wrapped up in it. But they said I'm out. I'm leaving all that behind me. You need to go." She pointed to the door we'd come through. "My break's over."

"I know you're not going to listen to me, but maybe ask around about a woman named Lola Cox. Find out what happened to her when the Order promised her something."

Retreating, I made my way back to the front of the restaurant. The door opened as I reached for the handle and Jacquie came striding through. Our gazes met and I nodded for her to follow me to an unoccupied corner.

"I thought I was handling this conversation," Jacquie said in a hushed tone.

"I should have texted, sorry. We had another attack. It happened here which made me think of Gabrielle. She all but admitted to taking Richard's magic. Though she wouldn't tell me how. She insists that it was one last favor for the Order before they let her leave."

Jacquie shook her head. "Obviously she's scared and thinks talking to the Order's number one enemy is likely to get her killed."

"Trying to leave their ranks is more likely to end that way," I muttered. "I didn't push her hard. I don't know, maybe a part of me feels bad for her."

"Are you sure that's the problem?"

"I can't have sympathy for her?" I retorted.

"She is involved in attacking people in your community. Shouldn't that make you furious?"

"I'm mad, of course I am. But right now, I need to keep things in check. I don't know how they're doing this and until I can figure that out, I don't know how to stop it."

"So you map where everyone's been and see if there's any overlap."

"Both attacks have happened in very public places; an all-day breakfast diner and a hole-in-the-wall North End Italian restaurant ... nowhere near each other from what I can gather. They probably aren't dumb enough to attack in someone's home or at headquarters. The amount of magic in either place is enough to make things go sideways."

"So maybe you institute a quarantine for everyone on the Council," Jacquie suggested.

It made sense. Moreover I had no idea how I would enforce it. I couldn't babysit a room full of adults and their families in addition to solving the threat to my people at the same time. "They wouldn't go for it."

"That's a lame excuse and you know it, Ezri."

I nudged her arm. "Can we talk about this some-where else? I don't need Gabrielle overhearing us. She may think she's free of the Order, but we both know that isn't the case.

"Couldn't you have tried that whole memory walk thing you did with the girls?" Jacquie held the door for me, and I stepped into the crisp evening air.

"I've done that twice today already. Plus I tried to go through someone else's memory in my own head. I need time to recharge first." A tiny voice in the back of my head reminded me that I had access to an entire lineage's worth of magical power boosts hanging around my neck. However, I wasn't going to burn through the magic imbued in the pendant unless I had no other choice.

We started down the crowded sidewalks, dodging lines of people as we approached North Station. "I paid our old buddy Taggart a visit on my way here like you asked," Jacquie said once the crowds around the station dissipated. "As expected, he claims to have no knowledge of what's happening."

"Bastard."

"He did let one thing slip, though," she replied.

I stopped walking and moved to bar her path forward. "You can't just stop there!"

"He mentioned that I should ask you since you've got experience."

"Has he taken one too many punches to the head in lock-up? I've never done anything like that."

Jacquie arched an eyebrow at me. "Hold up, isn't that what you did to Kevin Ellery?"

"No that was different. I ..." *Was it different?* I'd taken Kevin's magic, pulled it out of every fiber of his being in order to save him from the spell turning his magic inward against him. It's the same spell I still carried within me. Except I didn't intend to strip it out of his bloodline. I hadn't been in touch with his mother, but she hadn't used her magic in years. She'd told me as much when we first met.

"Okay, maybe it's similar but Jacquie, I don't know how I did that."

"Maybe you should figure it out."

No pressure.

SEPTEMBER 18, 2017

SEVEN

J.T. lay in bed beside me, snoring softly. My phone's display read 1:07 a.m., still I couldn't sleep. I stared up at the unfamiliar ceiling, trying to will myself to fall back asleep. I tried to go over what I remembered about pulling Kevin's magic out of him, but both it and sleep eluded me.

"I believe this is one of those instances where asking for assistance would be helpful," a soft female voice said from the doorway.

I rolled over to find the figure of Theodora Harrow—my ancestor—standing there. She smiled at me kindly, but with a touch of exasperation. Before she'd pointed me in the right direction with the kidnappings. Maybe she could give me a hint in the right direction this time, too. I crawled out of bed so as not to wake J.T. and together Theodora and I moved to the living room. She looked around at the new surroundings.

"You couldn't have popped in with that little nugget of wisdom before now? I've been laying there for hours," I grumbled.

"Well, you are a clever and resourceful young woman. Perhaps I wanted to see what you could learn on your own," she answered.

"Yeah, well clearly your confidence in me was misplaced, because I don't actually know what I did to Kevin." I pushed hair out of my face and began to pace among the boxes strewn around the room, my breathing starting to pick up. I could feel my heart starting to beat faster in my chest as my frustration rose.

"Child, be still and look at me," Theodora commanded.

I stopped moving and locked eyes with her. I watched her inhale and exhale in a steady, slow rhythm despite the fact she wasn't really alive. I mirrored her breathing and with each breath, my heart slowed back to normal, the anxiety ratcheted back down to manageable levels.

"Sorry," I mumbled.

She closed the gap between us and took my face in her hands. "You carry the weight of the world on your shoulders, my dear. For that I feel I must beg your forgiveness. But you also carry great strength in you."

I nodded. "I know. Our family magic."

"There's more to it than you understand. But that's for another time. Let us turn our minds to the problem at hand ... The young gargoyle."

"I told you, I'm stuck."

"Describe what happened," Theodora said. "The details of what your surroundings and your magic felt like."

I stepped out of range of her touch and settled on the couch. I closed my eyes and let my magic build up around me. It wasn't exactly the same as a trip down memory lane, not like I'd been doing all day, but it was enough of a boost to help me recall what happened. "We were in the Public Garden. It was a little cold, but a pretty clear night. It was after midnight. Eleanor helped me create a binding circle to talk to Kevin."

"What did your magic feel like?"

"Feel like? I'm not sure. I told Kevin to try to use his magic. We were going to try and redirect what it was doing to him. I didn't mean to strip him of his powers."

"No, you had intention to change what was. That is a starting point," Theodora replied.

"I'd gone in *intending* to turn him back to human from stone. Nowhere did I think, gee let's just take away his magical identity while we're at it."

"The magic that bound him in stone was made of his magic, correct?"

"Yes. But—"

"And you intended to remove the stone from his person?"

"Yeah. But I didn't want to hurt him," I replied.

"I believe on the whole, you did not harm him as you think. He thrives?"

I shrugged. "He's in prison. I wouldn't call that thriving, but he's human and that's what he wanted."

"So, you had intended to take the magic within him away so it no longer kept him encased in stone."

I considered her words slowly. "I ... I guess in a way, I did. But, even assuming that's true, I didn't want to affect his entire bloodline and that's exactly what the Order is doing. They're stripping whole families of their magic, their connection, from children all the way to the middle aged and elderly," I explained, thinking of Richard's mother.

"And that may be the difference in how the spell manifests. Perhaps you would like to confirm whether your actions had the same result?"

"I'm not calling Mrs. Ellery in the middle of the night," I answered.

"Ez? Who are you talking to?" J.T. stood in the doorway to the bedroom looking sleepy and so adorable.

"No one," I lied. I wasn't sure he'd understand the magical assist. I knew Desmond would be pissed if he found out about this special family connection and that I'd shared it with someone other than him first.

"It's the middle of the night. Come to bed. You need to get some rest."

"Couldn't sleep so I came out here to think. Sorry, I didn't want to wake you up," I told him, leaving the couch and wrapping my arms around his torso.

"You know I can tell when you're lying, Ez. You were talking to someone. Who was it?"

"I ..." I trusted J.T. After everything I'd put him through, I knew he deserved the truth. "Sometimes I get visits from dead relatives."

"Uh ... Explain, because it just sounded like you're saying you're haunted by ghosts. Magic can do a lot of amazing things, but I'm pretty sure raising the dead is out of even your wheelhouse."

He'd clearly never met a necromancer before. "They aren't ghosts exactly." I touched the pentacle around my neck. "You know this was passed down through my family since the Witch Trials, right?"

"Yeah. Your mom gave it to you on your birthday before she died." I felt his back stiffen as the words left his mouth.

"Well, it turns out that it contains a little bit of magic from everyone who has worn the pendant."

"Everyone? Even your mother?"

Sadness washed over me. "Yes. They can boost my magic sometimes. It's partly how I managed to stop the Order at the last Equinox. She and Eleanor Pruitt sacrificed the last bits of their magic to break the druid resurrection."

"So, who were you talking to just now?"

I looked to where my unexpected guest had been. She'd disappeared now. "Theodora Harrow. She pointed me in the right direction with the kidnappings. I guess she thought it best to share a few suggestions on how to handle this stolen magic business."

He followed my gaze, but he saw nothing only empty space. "Is she still here?"

"Yes and no. Her magic still exists in the pentacle, but no, she's not here in the room anymore."

"I've never heard of magic acting like that before. Being able to leave a piece of yourself behind."

"Me either, but I'll take all the help I can get. We had a chat about what I did to Kevin. She made me realize even though I hadn't intended to take Kevin's magic away, I had wanted to take away the spell that was keeping him confined in stone. And that was his own magic. I couldn't break that spell and leave him access to any magic at all."

"You think that's what the Order is doing?"

"Maybe. I mean, Taggart's part of the spell at least, ended up inside of me. It had to go somewhere, because its intention was to latch on to someone else's magic and turn it against them."

I started pacing again, trying to work through the

problem. "I need to see if Kevin's mom still has access to her abilities. But even if she doesn't, it doesn't explain where Yvette or Richard's magic *went.*"

"It still exists somewhere. I mean, it has to. You can't destroy it."

"A container!" The pieces began falling into place in my head.

"Again, you're going to need to explain," J.T. prompted.

"It was something Gabrielle said to me earlier. She said she was given instructions and that she had to deliver the stolen magic. She didn't elaborate on how though. What if they had some sort of container that they stored the magic in and brought it back to the Order?"

"It's possible." He grabbed me by the wrist and pulled me in close. "But you really need rest. Come back to bed."

I wanted to argue, but the soothing sweetness of honey tickled my nose and I failed to stifle a yawn. Under other circumstances, I'd argue with him for using magic on me without my consent. Although I was already too tired to argue as he pulled me close beneath the covers and kissed my cheek.

"You're going to solve this, Ez. But only if you take care of yourself," he whispered as the world melted into darkness.

EIGHT

A loud trumpeting sound roused me from a dreamless sleep. I swatted at the sound as the grogginess faded. J.T. sat up beside me, holding my phone in his hand.

My brain took a minute to associate the sounds with Dad's ringtone, but then the last dregs of sleep fled as I snatched the phone from J.T.'s hand. "Dad, are you okay?"

"I'm fine, honey. Why, what's going on?"

"It's a little hard to explain. What's up?"

"Well, I figured it would be more polite to call you instead of barging in. I brought coffee and pastries."

"What?"

"You invited me over today to help you look through your mother's books, remember?"

I gave a shaky laugh. "Right. Of course. Give me

like five minutes." I ended the call and looked to J.T. "He brought breakfast."

"Let's not keep him waiting then."

Five minutes on the dot later, I pulled open the front door and ushered Dad inside, snatching the coffee cup with my name on it. It was strong and heavy on the sugar, just like I preferred. *When did he learn my coffee order?*

"So, seeing as I'm here, why don't you tell me what's going on that's so complicated to explain?"

J.T. disappeared into the kitchen, leaving Dad and I standing in the living room, staring awkwardly at one another over to-go coffee cups. "Uh, well, members of the Council are losing their magic. Actually it's being stolen, stripping entire bloodlines. I think I might have an idea how they're doing it, but nothing yet as to the why."

"I see. And I'm assuming the people behind this are the same ones your mother died to protect you from?"

"The Order of Samael," I replied with a nod.

"I know you're supposed to be the Savior. I'm all for you being a strong, independent woman, but you're still my little girl and I don't want you getting hurt."

"I can take care of myself, Dad. These guys have tried and failed to take me out. They're going to fail again."

Dad sighed and bowed his head. Maybe he was

accepting defeat. "I know I'm not a part of this community, but I want to help in whatever way I can," Dad took a long pull from his coffee.

"Good, because I'm going to need you to do some research like you promised." I snatched a pastry from the bag and stuffed it in my mouth.

"Why do I get the feeling you're going to abandon me to do all the book work?" Dad's lips quirked into a smile.

I swallowed. "Because I am. I have to pay a visit to someone to see if a theory pans out. And, as much as it pains me to admit it, we need to convene another emergency meeting of the Council and come up with a game plan. So far they've attacked twice in public places where they could easily blend in. We're already down two of thirteen council members in a day. We need to figure out a contingency plan to keep the rest of the members and their families safe."

"I've already called my parents and told them to stay indoors for now," J.T. said, returning from the kitchen with plates and utensils. *What a gentleman?*

"Good." His family had been on the Council since before either of us were born. Not quite as long as the Pruitts and the Harrows, but still a respectable tenure.

"How at risk are you?" Dad's smile faded, replaced by worry lines.

"I'm always a target, Dad. That's what being the

Savior means. But I don't think they'd come at me directly again. Like I said, they tried that once and failed. Besides, light magic still has a slight advantage over them for a few more days, until the Equinox balances things out again." *Until we start the back-slide to the Winter Solstice and then their power boosts.*

"Just promise me you'll try to be careful. You're all I've got left in this world, Ezri."

"I'll be careful," I told him. I meant it, too. Though I had my doubts the world would cooperate.

Having finished my pastry and coffee, I headed for the front door with J.T. hot on my heels. "Are you sure you don't want me to come with you?'

"I'm capable of visiting Kevin's mom on my own," I answered.

"Your dad has a point. If they are targeting the Council, that puts a bigger bullseye on your back.'

"I know you're trying to help and watch out for me. I love that about you, but you're just as much of a target as me. So is Desmond. You need to lay low like you told your parents to do. The less access they have to us, the safer we'll be."

NINE

"You really didn't have to come with me," I told Jacquie as we pulled up in front of Mrs. Ellery's house.

"My partner needed me. I'm here. Have there been any more attacks?" She replied and climbed out of the passenger seat.

"Not that I've heard. I'm really hoping that what I did to Kevin is different than what they're doing now."

"But if it's not, isn't that better in a way?" Jacquie let me take the lead up to the front door.

"How do you figure?"

"If it's the same thing you did, can't you just reverse engineer it and undo their spell?"

"I don't know. Gabrielle said that she had to deliver the magic somewhere. Implying it had to be a tangible thing and that means the stolen magic exists somewhere. I can't just recreate it from the natural magic around us. It wouldn't be *theirs*."

"Oh ..." Jacquie looked vaguely annoyed by my explanation. Or maybe it was that the conversation made it abundantly clear she was an outsider in all of this.

I knocked twice on the door and waited. Mrs. Ellery appeared several minutes later. Unlike the last time we'd crossed paths, she was bright-eyed, if a bit startled.

"Detectives, is something wrong?"

"We're hoping not, but we'd like to come in and talk for a few minutes if you have time," I answered.

"Is it about Kevin?" Worry lines framed the corners of her eyes and mouth.

"In a way, yes. Please, it's better if we talk inside," I insisted.

She stepped aside and I moved from the short entryway to the living room. It was far cleaner and brighter than when we'd been here looking for information on her missing son six months ago.

"Have you been to see Kevin lately?" I started off easy.

"I go twice a month on Tuesdays. He's hanging in there. That nice girl, Kayla, visits him every week." Color drained from her face. "Oh God, has something happened to Kevin?"

"No, your son is fine," Jacquie reassured her.

"Actually, I need to ask you about your magic," I said, making direct eye contact with Mrs. Ellery.

"My what?" I could tell she was feigning ignorance for Jacquie's sake.

"She knows the truth. You can speak openly," I said.

"I told you before that I haven't used it in a long time," she sighed.

"I remember, but I need to know if you still have your abilities."

Her brow furrowed in confusion. "Why wouldn't it still be there?"

"Well, the people who hurt your son are attacking other people in the community and it's affecting relatives. In order to save Kevin, I had to take his magic. I need to know if you were affected, too," I explained, trying to keep the details just vague enough to keep the wider community in the dark that their governing body was under attack.

"That's awful. I ... I don't know how I can help you, though.'

"You could do some magic for us," Jacquie said.

I snorted at the comment. "Sorry." I cleared my throat to regain my composure. "She's right though. You could do a small spell just enough that I can pick up on your signature to make sure it's still there."

"My signature?" Yet, more confusion furrowed her brow.

"Everyone has their talents. The universe

thought it would be great for me to have the ability to sniff out magic," I answered.

"Fascinating. I knew magic had a smell, but I never realized it mattered. I guess I wasn't around other people enough to realize that magic didn't smell the same."

"What does it smell like for you? Knowing that will help me pinpoint if it's still there," I probed.

"Saffron," she said, her cheeks flushing a little.

"Great." I looked around the room. "Why don't we try something small? Move that picture on the mantle over to the table."

"Seems easy enough," she muttered and closed her eyes.

I watched her breathing even out to become slow and rhythmic. She pressed her lips into a firm line in concentration. At first, nothing happened and beads of sweat formed on my hairline. Maybe I had done exactly what the Order did to Yvette and Richard. Then, the fragrant scent of saffron filled the room and the picture frame zipped through space landing on the table.

"I think that answers that question," Jacquie offered.

Relief washed over me, and I pulled Mrs. Ellery into a bear hug. "Thank you. This helps," I whispered in her ear.

"I just moved a picture. I didn't do anything earth shattering."

"You did more than you know." I hadn't messed up Kevin's family line which meant the spell I'd done wasn't anything like the Order. While that gave me some sense of absolution, it still left me with no way of knowing how they'd done it or what they were doing with the magic once it was taken.

"Thank you again. The next time you see Kevin, tell him the Savior says hi," I said and stepped back.

"He'll be glad to hear you're checking up on him."

Jacquie and I retreated to the car. We sat with the key in the ignition, but the engine off for a solid minute before Jacquie nudged my shoulder. "You have that look like you're trying to sort things out without including the rest of us."

"Sorry. I keep thinking about what Gabrielle said. And the spell I saw in Yvette's memory, it felt tangible."

"So, let's pay our waitress friend another visit."

"She won't talk to me," I replied.

"You remember that boyfriend of hers? How he insisted he had a medical card for all that pot he reeked of?"

"I do."

"How much you want to bet he's growing more than he's supposed to?"

I nodded. "And you think maybe bringing Gabrielle in since she's probably on the lease might scare her into talking."

"At the very least it gives us cover for why we need to talk to her."

"Let's do it."

TEN

Tracking Gabrielle down wasn't difficult, and she stayed silent as we brought her back to the station. No one questioned us as we led her into an interrogation room.

"This is harassment. That stuff isn't even mine," Gabrielle spat the moment she sat down.

"Your name is on the lease so we can charge you just the same as your boyfriend," I said and sat down across from her. "Or, you can talk to me, answer my questions truthfully, and we let you walk out of here."

"I told you yesterday, I'm not talking." Her gaze darted to Jacquie who sat stone-faced beside me.

"And yet I know there's more to the story than what you gave me yesterday. I know you think the Order is going to let you walk away from all this, but you're wrong. They've lied to you again, Gabrielle," I said. I hoped a little bad cop might force her to open up.

"You don't know anything about them," she muttered, leaning forward as if to share her deepest, darkest secrets with us.

"Then tell me who they are. Help me get to know them."

"You want to take them down, but they will just keep coming back. It's what they do. Your kind tried to wipe them out during the Witch Trials and it just made them stronger.'

"Everything has a balance, Gabrielle. Even them. And in case you're keeping score, they're zero for two right now when they've gone up against me. Not great odds if you ask me.'

"They only want to be free. To use their gifts as they were intended," Gabrielle said sharply.

"They're using those gifts to murder innocent people. They tortured little girls, because they had information that might be useful and left them with mental scars that may never heal. So, don't you dare sit there and tell me they're redeemable," I snapped.

Jacquie leaned over and whispered, "Can't you just go in her head like you did with the girls?"

"I got away with that then and yesterday, but I can't keep doing it." I understood why it had wiped Desmond out so much back in June. I focused back on Gabrielle. "Please, if you truly want to be free from them, help me stop whatever they're planning.

Help me dismantle them so they can't go after you or anyone else again."

"I told you, they put some sort of instructions in my head, I acted on them and that's all. I wasn't even in control of my own body."

"Do you know if the spell is still there?"

"I don't feel it anymore, no."

"Did you use your own magic or was it fueled by someone else?"

"I have no idea. How would I even know that?'

I shook my head and pressed the pad of my right index finger to the sandalwood charm around my neck. I inhaled and let the charm wash away the saffron of Mrs. Ellery's magic. Lucky for me, Gabrielle had done the spell less than twenty-four hours ago so the magic would still be fresh. I hadn't picked up on it before, but I caught the hint of vinegar—on her. The same scent as in Yvette's memory. *Was that there when I talked to her yesterday?* It had to have been, but maybe my senses had been thrown off by all of the spices used in an Italian restaurant's kitchen. I picked up the faintest hint of limes.

"Does your magic smell like citrus?"

"Limes, why?" Gabrielle answered.

"Because, you used a little of your own magic to fuel whatever spell this was, but it primarily came from the person who gave you the instructions. I need to know everything you remember about what you were told. Was there a time-delay on the spell? Did it only kick on once you confirmed the person you were targeting was present?"

Gabrielle rubbed at her temples. "Someone sent me a name and a picture. There was a note that said he came in every Sunday and when I saw him, I would know what to do."

Progress. "Did you meet with anyone before then? How did they give you the magical instructions to act?" I knew technology could be affected by magic—I'd seen what it could do firsthand—but this felt personal. Something that had to have been done face to face.

Gabrielle shook her head and buried her face in her hands. I could hear soft sobs coming from her as I sat there, waiting for an answer. As much as I didn't want to alienate her and push her into not talking to us, I also needed answers. So, I stood up, the sound of the chair legs scraping against the floor drawing her attention.

"If you're not going to help, we'll just have to book you for the drug charges and see where things go from there."

I had my hand on the doorknob when she reached out a hand in my direction. "Wait. I'll tell you what I know, okay? But you have to promise me it won't trace back to me." She wiped at her eyes. "I did like you said and asked around about Lola. Word on the street is she took her own life rather than talk.

She may have done the deed herself, but I don't want to end up dead."

I returned to the chair. "Good choice. And we'll keep your name out of it. Now, start talking."

Gabrielle pushed hair out of her face and dried her eyes. "I don't know why they're doing all this now. I just know they said it had to happen. So they gave me that man's name and picture."

"Via text or hard copy?" Jacquie chimed in.

Gabrielle pulled out her phone and passed it over. There was a message with Richard's name and the picture looked to have been taken while he was out and about, unaware that he was being followed. The message beneath the picture said 'wait for further instructions.' The message was dated three days ago.

"You get the text, then what happens," I asked.

"This guy I didn't know showed up at the restaurant on my break Saturday. I knew he was from the Order because of the brand. I don't know, maybe he joined up recently or something. All I know is he took my hands, gave me a necklace and told me that when I saw the man, I'd know what to do."

"Gabrielle, this is very important, when he took your hand, could you feel his magic at all?"

"Maybe. I was just so scared, you know?"

I did. I hadn't had occasion to meet this jackass in person, but he was damn menacing in memory.

"So, you took the necklace and when Richard came in the next day, you took his magic?"

She nodded mutely; her fingers clasped tightly in front of her. "That's all I know. Like I said, I don't really remember using my own magic. It was like whatever he did to me, took over and acted on its own."

"What happened to the necklace he gave you?" I gestured to her bare throat. Could the necklace have been what was used to store Richard's magic? I didn't recall seeing one in Yvette's memory, but I hadn't witnessed the whole thing.

"I got another text saying to drop it off at a pawn shop. Tell the owner it was a family heirloom and I just needed to leave it there for safe keeping."

"You happen to remember the name of the shop or where it's located?" Jacquie asked, sliding a pen and notepad across the table.

Gabrielle bit her lower lip before scribbling something down. "I swear, that's all I know. I dropped it off late last night. That's all I had to do."

"So, they only gave you one person to target?" I had a feeling the answer was "yes," but I needed to hear her confirm it.

"That's all I got," she replied.

"If you get another text like this, you contact me immediately." I slid my business card to her. "You understand?"

Gabrielle pocketed the card, but rolled her eyes at me. "Whatever ... Can I go now?"

Jacquie and I exchanged a look before I gestured to the door. "You're free to go."

Gabrielle marched out of the interview room and I leaned back in the chair. Jacquie was hunched over studying Gabrielle's scribble. "Magical pawn shop? Is that really a thing?"

"Wouldn't surprise me. I'm tempted to run it by an underground contact before we make any moves, but he can be a little ... prickly."

"Ah yes, your scary bartender," Jacquie mused.

"He's not all that scary. He just doesn't like the fact I messed up his bar."

"I don't trust him though," Jacquie said and stood up.

"He came through last time," I reminded her.

"Yeah, because we had leverage over him and he's not stupid. By now, he's renewed those licenses. I'm pretty sure whatever good will you had, went up in smoke when you trashed the place."

Jonathan owned the only bar I was aware of in the city that catered specifically to people with magic. I had no doubt Notre Dame saw the occasional normal person, but it was also a common hangout of lower level Order members. I understood why Jacquie didn't trust him and she wasn't wrong. He wasn't my biggest fan. Despite that I'd followed through on my word that the Authority would pay for the damage Lola and her friends had caused. I hadn't gone there intending to start a literal firefight with a guy who threw very real fireballs. Still the situation had devolved into it and the bar had taken damage. Agreeing to foot the bill was the only way I got Jonathan to agree to let me interrogate Lola. Before I could say anything else, my phone rang with an incoming call from Dad.

"Give me a minute," I told Jacquie before stepping into the hall and taking the call. "Hey, Dad. How are things in the land of old books?"

"Fine. Nothing jumps out at me about stealing magic, but I'll keep looking. I just wanted to check up on you. You left pretty quick after I got here."

"Yeah, sorry. I had to follow up on something."

"And I'm guessing that something isn't anything you could share with your dad."

A wave of guilt washed over me. I'd spent so long keeping him out of my life, because of magic. I still found it hard to include him, even though our relationship was in the best place it had been since my mother's death. "A few months ago, I did a spell to reverse a curse put on a guy and it ended up stripping him of his powers. We needed to know if it was the same thing happening to the Council now. Turns out, it isn't. So that's good. But it also doesn't entirely help us solve the problem."

"Well, I know you'll figure it out. It is curious that it is affecting entire families."

"In a way, it makes sense. Magic always passes through the maternal line. If your intention is to steal an entire family's magical ability, I guess you could just target one person and have it act as a ripple effect." Making me wonder if Desmond were attacked, would it ripple all the way to me? Jacquie stepped out of the interview room and jingled her car keys to let me know where she was headed.

"Have you thought about testing out your theory?" Dad's voice pulled me back to the conversation.

"What do you mean?"

"Well, you know what you did with the curse. And you know what the end result is for what they're doing now. Can't you try to recreate it?"

ELEVEN

Shortly before noon, Jacquie and I sat in her car across the street from Kenny's Pawn Brokerage out near Fenway. The sign on the door read 'out to lunch' except I caught movement within. I could make out two male figures through windows.

"I need to get closer," I said with my hand on the door handle when Jacquie grabbed my other arm.

"If Gabrielle's intel is right and the Order is using this as a drop, they're bound to know your face. You may be anonymous to the rest of the world, but to them you are Public Enemy Number One. You can't get close. Let me."

"You can't just walk in there. We don't know what's going on in there and for all we know, they know who you are, too. I mean they did go after your niece."

"Need I remind you; I've been doing this a lot

longer than you. I know how to go undercover. I'll go in and do low-key surveillance. Nothing that we'd need a warrant for. Just snap some quick photos, see what I can pick up."

"Okay, fine. But you'll need something to take in with you," I reminded her and reached up to undo the clasp of my necklace.

"I got it covered. Just stay put and if anyone else shows up, try to get pictures so we can run them through the system."

I didn't like being sidelined, especially when this was all about magic—my domain. Jacquie was the more seasoned officer between us and I knew she was a damn good cop. I just prayed her appearance didn't scream law enforcement when she walked through the door. The way she walked and carried herself after years of concealing a gun on the job were hard to hide.

I chewed my bottom lip as my nerves started to fray the longer Jacquie was gone. I could just make out her outline standing behind the man on the customer side of the counter, but I hated not knowing what they were saying or doing.

"Don't you even think about going over there," a voice I hadn't heard since I was five or six years old said from the backseat.

I turned to find my grandmother—or rather the manifestation of her magic—sitting there donning aviator sunglasses and a blouse with ridiculously large shoulder pads. "Nice look. But, how are you here? You sacrificed yourself in the fight against the Order in March."

She waved a hand dismissively. "I was always the spitting image of my mother. That's who you saw that day."

I'd never met my great grandmother but took her at her word. After all, she couldn't be here if it had really been her who made the sacrifice back then.

"You need to work on relying on other people, sweet girl."

"I'm trying, believe me. I just hate that she's in there without any back-up. Without having magic she's not equipped to fight these kinds of bad guys. Not like I am."

"Ezzie, you're a good girl. I'm sure you're an excellent partner, but you need to have faith that the world's gonna keep turning even if you can't save the day every single time."

She was the only person who ever called me that. It hadn't stuck for the rest of the family and I was both a little sad and grateful. Yet, in that moment, it warmed me to know she still had my back. "Did you ever think it could have been you or Mom that was supposed to be the Savior?"

"Every day. I was a little selfish, truth be told. I prayed for a boy. I thought maybe it was wrong. Or maybe it would be Eleanor's line."

"Yeah, we were wrong with that one. She always knew it would be Theodora's line."

"Hmmm. Heard that one straight from the horse's mouth, huh?"

"Actually, I did." I studied her features, so much like what I imagined my mother would have looked like if she'd hit middle age before dying, "How come you haven't visited before now?"

"Because, darling, you haven't needed me." She pointed to my chest with a knowing smirk. "We can tell what you need when you need it. Ain't magic grand."

"Yes, it is pretty amazing."

After a pause, Grandma pointed to the center console where I'd set my phone. "You're going to want to check that."

I looked down at the screen to see an incoming text from Jacquie telling me to call her. "How'd you ..." I looked up, but Grandma was gone. I hit Jacquie's name on my contacts.

"Please tell me you found it. This is the fifth shop I've been to," Jacquie said in an exasperated tone.

"You need back-up?" The words were out of my mouth before I realized she needed to make whatever ruse she was playing out appear more real.

"Oh, thank God!" Her voice softer as she said, "My daughter just found the ring. Thanks for your help."

I could hear the bell above the door ring over the phone line as I watched the man who'd been inside leave, shoving his hands into his pockets. I flipped to my camera and snapped a few pictures. It certainly looked like the man who'd stolen Yvette's magic. Jacquie followed thirty seconds later and crossed the street. I slipped down below the window in case she was being watched. She climbed behind the wheel and pulled away from the sidewalk without saying a word.

"Please tell me you got something useful?" I prodded.

"I'll fill you in when we get where we're going. Please just tell me you got a clear picture of that guy's face."

We ended up walking the Common, finally settling on a bench away from any other groups of people. There was the possibility of an eavesdropper, but it was less likely in the middle of the day.

"The guy in front of me told the cashier he was there to pick up a necklace his daughter had left there for safe keeping the night before. He showed him a picture of the necklace on his phone," Jacquie explained once we'd settled in.

"So, he picked up the necklace. Any money exchanged? Did the cashier verify his identity in any way?" I asked around a mouthful of food.

"I couldn't tell. The way he was holding the phone it could have been at an angle to show off a brand on his wrist. Or maybe he'd been in before so they knew they could trust each other. The necklace was in a clear pouch. It looked to be pewter with some sort of crystal at the center. It looked almost like it could have been a knock-off opal with the color." She passed me her phone. "Didn't get great pictures, but it's better than nothing."

I enlarged the image of the pouch with the necklace inside. It had the same color as the spell I'd seen in progress from Yvette's memory. If I had to venture a guess, this was what her contained magic looked like. "I don't know that guy's name, but he's the same one who held the girls and took Yvette's magic. He's a major player. We ID him and we have a shot at stopping this." My phone buzzed with an incoming text from J.T.

"Third attack."

My heart skipped a beat and for a minute my lungs forgot how to breathe. Black spots danced in my vision and I had to set the phone aside to regain control of my body.

"What's wrong?" Jacquie's voice sounded far away.

"There's been another attack. I don't know any of the details, but we are running out of time. They're escalating and if they keep up this pace, there's going to be no one left on the Council by the end of the week."

TWELVE

I was beginning to hate the drive to Headquarters. Moreover I hated being on the offensive. Dad's idea to reverse engineer the spell was sounding better and better. Though we also knew whoever had the stolen magic in their possession was on their way to the pawn shop for a drop. From Jacquie's report, Mr. Vinegar had only picked up one item. What's more if the attack had just happened, we might have a window of opportunity to get the necklace and restore the magic to it's rightful owner. At least then it would feel like I was doing something useful. Something specific to protect the people who relied on me.

The group hadn't bothered to gather in the meeting room on the second floor. They'd all crammed into the library and expressions were somber as I walked in. I searched the faces and took a head count.

We were down to eleven people, which made sense since I'd sent both Yvette and Richard home yesterday.

"Who is it?" I made eye contact with J.T. and then Desmond. Both looked clear-eyed, if a bit haggard. At least they were still safe.

"Shawna Mont Claire," Belladonna answered from the back of the group.

"And we've confirmed her family has been affected?" I turned my attention to the healer.

"She was more concerned with her child."

I gripped the edge of the table as I recalled seeing her yesterday. She hadn't gotten up much, because she was eight months pregnant. "Did something happen to the baby?"

"She isn't sure, but she said that she hadn't felt the baby move in an hour or two. Her husband took her for an emergency appointment with her midwife," Belladonna answered.

"Okay. Well, we're getting closer to answers."

"Care to share with the rest of us?" Desmond's voice carried from the far side of the table.

I'd held onto the information as long as I could. "I don't want to scare anyone more than they already are, but the Order has a list of the Council members. I don't know when or how they came to have it, but that's irrelevant. The point is they do and as everyone has probably figured out by now, they're picking us off one family at a time."

"How are we supposed to protect ourselves if we don't know what's coming?" Agnes Phelps, a middle-aged woman with dark eyes and a constantly sour expression piped up. She'd always reminded me of an angry librarian.

"The attacks seem to be happening in public places that people frequent. So, I'd say try to stay inside as much as possible. So far, they've targeted the actual Council members, but they could change up their approach if they realize we're on to them."

"And what are you doing to undo what they've done?" Agnes quipped.

Her tone sounded like she was scolding me for returning a late library book and I bristled. "I'm working with my police contacts to track the man we think is responsible for Yvette's attack and who is organizing the others. We have some information on how the operation is being run and I'm working on a way to replicate what they're doing so I can reverse it. But I need everyone to be patient." I took a breath and squared my shoulders. "I know you're all looking to me, because I'm the Savior. Yet that doesn't mean I have all the answers. If you have any suggestions, I'm open to them."

A knock on the door interrupted the conversation. Jacquie stuck her head in and said, "I need to borrow you for a minute."

"Excuse me," I addressed the group and stepped

into the hallway. She held up her phone to show me a mug shot of Mr. Vinegar. "We got him."

I snatched the phone away and scrolled through the file. Reuben Wickham, current resident of Dorchester, had a list of charges dating back decades, mostly for assault and battery, and theft. He'd managed to stay out of prison which made me think he'd most likely used his own magic to his advantage somehow.

"Can we put some plain clothes officers on the pawn shop, have them scoop up this asshole if he shows again?"

Jacquie shook her head. "We'd need a warrant, probable cause. You know, all the stuff the law requires. Besides retrieving an item from a pawn shop isn't a crime unless it's stolen and we can't prove it was."

"Come on, Jacquie, we know that what the necklace contained was stolen."

"And you want to walk into the captain's office and spill the beans about magic? Bringing a single FBI agent into the fold is one thing, but you wouldn't have any proof to wave in front of Beech's nose," Jacquie retorted.

I hated that she was right. "We need to get this guy off the street, Jacquie. He's the one who hurt Neveah, remember?"

Jacquie's gaze narrowed and I took an involuntary step backward. "Oh, I remember just fine, Ezri. I want to nail this son-of-a-bitch too, but we can't use police resources to nail him for things that aren't technically crimes."

The door to the library opened and Desmond stepped out to join us. "Sorry to interrupt, but I needed to tell you something."

"I'm all ears."

"The people who've been attacked first, they came onto the Council more recently. It seems they're picking off the less senior members first. Maybe it's a coincidence or maybe it means something more. I think your idea of trying to replicate what they are doing is smart, but I don't think you're going to get many volunteers."

"She's got one," J.T. replied from the doorway.

"I can't ask you to do that," I told him.

"You didn't ask. I offered. Besides, I trust you and I know you're not doing it alone." He winked and I sent up a silent prayer that Desmond didn't catch the gesture.

I'd let J.T. in on my secret communications with my family members from beyond the grave. I wasn't sure I was ready to have Desmond know that little fact. I could just hear him demanding to know why my mother's magical essence hadn't simply filled me in on what happened right after it occurred and saved him from a decade of guilt. Plus, I suspected despite my cousin's many virtues, he'd be a little jealous that I had yet another magical step-up on him.

"Okay, fine," I relented. "But we're doing it at home where we have privacy and I can set up some extra precautions. Also, I think picking up an early dinner isn't the worst idea to thank Dad for digging through things all day. He was the one who suggested replicating the spell."

"I always knew he was a smart man," J.T. said with a smile.

"I'm coming over, too." Desmond interjected. "I'm not letting you do this without a safety net. I know you've got a lot of power Ez, but something like this is dangerous and we have no idea what it could do to both of you."

"Fine, but you better let that new wife of yours know that you won't be home for a while."

THIRTEEN

Three hours of failure was bound to wear on a girl's confidence, and I slumped against the couch cushions in defeat, glowering at my dad, J.T., and Desmond standing opposite me.

"We have to keep trying," J.T. insisted.

"I need a break, because this isn't working. I need to clear my head, regroup," I answered.

"While you two have been experimenting, Desmond filled me in on his theory," Dad said, handing me a cup of coffee and a slice of pizza.

"That they're picking off the newer members first? Well then, they should have come after me first. I'm definitely the newest."

"Savior status makes you special," Desmond said softly.

"Well, when he mentioned that, it triggered something I'd read in one of your mother's books."

He passed over a book. "It seems like the original plan was to have it be hereditary, but occasionally lines died out and so new families stepped in."

"So, what, you think we should just replace the people who've been affected?"

"Not necessarily. But we should check to see when Yvette, Shawna, and Richard's families joined the Council. If we can figure out when everyone joined, maybe we can predict who they'll go after next," Desmond replied.

"But I still don't understand why that would matter? Magical ability is all the same, isn't it?" I posed.

"Maybe not. I mean, you're the Savior for a reason. So you have to have a different level of magic within you," Desmond replied.

"But with everyone else, isn't it just the same?" I repeated.

"You should listen to him, he's a smart boy," Grandma said from across the room.

I glanced her way, not wanting to look crazy in front of my family and loved ones. "Just give me a minute," I said and headed for the bathroom. Grandma appeared sitting on the toilet next to me as I turned on the water in a pathetic attempt to obscure the conversation.

"You picked a really bad time to show up."

"I picked the exact right time, sweetheart. The time when you needed me. Look, Desmond's a smart boy. You should listen to him more. And your father. I know he's not magical, but I always liked him. Whether you believe it or not, he sought my blessing not your Grandpa's to marry your mother. He knew who held the real power in our family."

"That's great, but what are you doing here?" I repeated.

Grandma lowered her sunglasses to glare at me from atop the toilet seat. "Were you even listening to what he said about bloodlines?"

"Yes," I answered defiantly. "They're going after the newer bloodlines first."

"And?" She prompted.

"And, not everyone's magic is the same."

"Our family magic is different than most. We birthed a Savior after all. Haven't you ever wondered why it was our line?"

"Because there was a prophecy about it," I said.

"Be curious and question things, Ezzie. Why would our bloodline be so different, so much stronger?"

"I don't know."

"Then find out!"

A knock on the door made me jump and when I turned back, Grandma was gone. "You okay, Ez?" Desmond's voice came through the closed door.

"Yeah, be right there."

I studied my reflection in the mirror for a minute, taking Grandma's words to heart. What *did* make our bloodline so unique? Why was *I* the Savior? I left the bathroom to find Dad, J.T., and Desmond waiting for me in the living room.

"So, what was that about?" Dad looked only mildly surprised.

"It's better if you tell them," J.T. said.

No getting around it, now. "I was talking to Grandma," I said bluntly.

"Uh ... Your dead grandmother?" Dad's eyebrows shot up into his hairline.

"I thought she sacrificed herself," JT noted.

"Yeah, so did I. Turns out I was wrong. Look, don't freak out, but I kind of communicate with dead relatives sometimes."

"Which dead relatives?" Desmond's voice was soft, but his tone bore an edge, one I'd been expecting and fearing. That little bit of jealousy he'd always had about me being the Savior was showing a tinge.

"Grandma, Eleanor Pruitt, Theodora Harrow, and ... my mom." I couldn't meet his gaze as the last words left my lips.

"You saw your mother?" Dad's hands reached for me, but didn't make contact. Like he was afraid mentioning Mom would destroy all the progress we'd made.

"Yeah. It's complicated, but the best I can understand, each person in the family who wore this pendant imbued some of their magic into it before they died so a piece of them is still around until they choose to sacrifice it." I forced myself to look at Desmond. "That's how I was able to stop the Order back in March. With their help."

"And you didn't want us hearing a private conversation?" Dad asked.

"I didn't want you to think I was crazy."

"You're not crazy, Ezri. I'm glad the last time you saw your mom wasn't in the video she recorded," Desmond added.

"Me, too." I sucked in a breath. "Anyway, Grandma told me we need to figure out why our bloodline is so different from everyone else. I mean, assuming that she's right."

"I think she might be. Your dad was showing us a journal entry about new magical bloodlines emerging over the years. It's how the Authority selected its Council members when the original bloodlines died out," J.T. explained.

I turned to Dad. "You're just full of good ideas today aren't you?"

"I do try."

"Show me the entries," I said.

Dad passed over a leather-bound volume opened to a particular page. I didn't recognize the writing. It was penned in a cramped, small script and I had to squint to read it.

The Journal of Dorothy Windsor, Council Archivist

22 July 1920

Our ranks have dwindled due to the Great War. Some among our remaining numbers fear that the Order may strike a blow as we and the world seek to recover from the many losses, mundane and otherwise, inflicted these last years.

But I have hope. I believe new blood will refresh our council, bring with it new perspectives and new ideas. It is my belief that new bloodlines are born all around us as others die out. For as we all know it to be true, magic cannot truly die. It lives on and must find a host to reside in. I believe, yet have no proof of such a theory, that these new bloodlines are weaker than those that endure. For there is some correlation between the skills of those that came before and the new practitioners who have joined our ranks in recent months. Their gifts are beautiful, but require more development than their predecessors. Further examination is required to prove my theory, but it does appear the longer a lineage is sustained, the greater the potential in later generations.

Dorothy Windsor didn't ring any bells in terms of our family line. "So, she's saying that the magic in one family dies out and when it remerges in someone else, it's less potent than the original."

"That's what it sounds like. We've skimmed the rest of her entries, but we can't tell if she ever managed to prove her theory," Desmond replied.

"If her theory's true though, that would mean the

magic the Order has already taken is weaker than yours or mine," I said, setting the journal aside. "That doesn't make sense. If they're trying to weaken us, the better plan of attack would be to take us out first, leaving the others vulnerable."

"You're not wrong. There's clearly something else going on that we don't understand. But this is more than we had an hour ago."

Dad cleared his throat. "There was something else in one of the books that talked about strength of ability, too," He turned around, rummaging through the neatly stacked piles of books with colorful little tabs marking different places.

I didn't remind him that these were centuries old and putting adhesive on the pages was probably a bad idea. He gently set them aside until he found the one he wanted, opening it to a tabbed page and passed it to me. I settled on the couch, studying the delicate script on the page. I recognized the handwriting as belonging to Theodora Harrow.

"Your grandmother is correct. Following the strength of our lineage is wise," Theodora said from beside me.

I looked up at her and realized everyone else was watching me. This was going to get very awkward—and tiresome—fast. "In case anyone's interested, Theodora Harrow just showed up and said that we're on the right track."

"What prompted her to show up?" J.T. wondered.

"This is her handwriting," I replied, focusing my attention back on Theodora's words.

It has been ten years since the passing of my dear sister, Eleanor, and yet I feel her presence with me daily. I have done the work she had requested of me. To shepherd the young and inexperienced in their gifts to the ways of the light, but I fear my efforts are not enough. I cannot put words to the feeling, other than I fear it is not enough. It is not that they lack the skills, but rather that the power flowing within their veins pales to that of my kin.

Many cannot trace the origins of their lineage so we may never learn where their bloodlines truly came from. And knowing where one's blood begins is the start of learning to truly control one's gift.

I turned to Theodora, my mouth slightly agape. "So, you knew this whole time that bloodlines mattered, and you couldn't have mentioned that at some point? Eleanor couldn't either?"

"You never posed the question."

"That's bullshit." The three men standing around me shared awkward glances, no doubt wondering what she'd said. I didn't have time to give them a play by play. "You could have told me bloodlines were significant three months ago. It could have changed things."

"I understand your anger, but it will do no one

any good to dwell on what could have been. Your focus should be the past, yes, but even farther back. To the place where our family magic was born."

"Great. Please tell me you know where that is."

Theodora faltered. "I do not know what name it holds in your time. It was the isle of the Celtic peoples during my time."

"How do you know that's where we came from? Weren't you and Eleanor born here in ... the colonies?"

"Yet our family kept detailed lineage to map our family's magical branches." She gave my cheek a pat. "Hurry now, my dear child. Time is running short."

And just like that, she vanished. I looked over at Desmond. "Gotta say, I think I preferred your ancestor to mine. At least Eleanor didn't withhold information just because I didn't ask for it."

"What'd she say?" J.T. interjected, moving to take the space Theodora had just occupied.

"That our family took great care to track our genealogy and she says our magic originated in the Isle of Celtic peoples."

"Ireland," Desmond said.

"It's a big place, not to mention we have no idea if it's in Northern Ireland or the Republic of Ireland," J.T. replied.

"We need to see what the genealogy says," I interjected and moved to the table, sifting through books until I realized that I didn't know if Dad had even grabbed all of the books.

"I didn't see anything like a genealogy in there," Dad said, placing a hand on my back. "I'm only going to say this once, as much as the idea of my daughter being an ocean away terrifies me, you being far away from these lunatics gives me some sense of relief.'

The farthest I'd been from home was a Spring Break trip up to Toronto my senior year of college. My passport certainly hadn't gotten much use since that time. Thankfully it was still valid. "Theodora, a little help?" I muttered.

The pentacle around my neck grew warm and the edge of a piece of parchment appeared out of the back of one of the books I'd already moved out of the way. "Thanks."

I eased it free and spread it out on the table. I didn't know if Mom had updated it when I was born, but my name was on there at the bottom right of the page in a script that matched all the other entries. For all I knew it was magically done. I traced the line connecting me to Mom to Grandma all the way back to Theodora and her sister Eleanor. I could see all the branches of their other children and their families who'd died out long ago to make up our family tree. It was a long line of women. As I passed each name, I could feel their magic rise to the surface of my senses, surrounding me with dozens of different smells from lavender to peaches and hay. I moved my finger beyond Theodora's name to her parents and further along up the tree. I could swear new scents hit me as the pad of my finger touched each name. *But the pendant had started with Eleanor and Theodora, not their ancestors, hadn't it?*

I reached the top of the genealogy with a woman's name I couldn't hope to pronounce. As I ran my fingers over the ink, air rushed out of my lungs and the condo fell away to be replaced by somewhere dark and earthy. A figure sat with their back to me some distance away. I couldn't speak or move. They didn't seem to want to move or notice me either. All at once, the earthy smell disappeared and I saw a flurry of images ending with an airport sign for Dublin before the living room rematerialized.

My balance abandoned me, and I fell backwards. Dark spots danced in my vision and I fought to get air into my lungs. The beautiful scents of honey and spearmint eased the fight my body was currently in until the world righted itself. I found myself sitting on the floor, J.T. on one side and Desmond on the other.

"What the hell was that?" J.T. demanded, pressing his fingers to my throat to check my pulse.

"I ... have no idea. But I think we need to start in Dublin."

"What happened?" Dad kept his distance. We'd never really talked about his involvement or lack thereof in Mom's magic. I guessed he knew enough to recognize something weird had just happened and that the guys with healer's skills were better equipped to help me.

"Somehow, I could feel each person's magic as I went back along the bloodline." *Well, not everyone.* "I could even sense something as I went back beyond Eleanor and Theodora. Then, I got to the top and it was like I wasn't here anymore. I was somewhere earthy and there was someone sitting there. It felt like they were waiting for me. I got flashes of hillsides and some other things, and a sign for Dublin airport."

Dad pulled out his phone and started tapping away. I wanted to ask what he was doing, but I figured he would tell me when he was done. "There's a flight that leaves in five hours. It has a couple layovers, but it gets you into Dublin tomorrow by 8:00 a.m. their time."

Layovers weren't ideal, but I was lucky to be able to get a flight this late. "Book it. I'll figure it out."

"How many seats are left on that flight?" J.T. asked, helping me up.

"Three left," Dad said. He tapped his phone screen a few more times in quick succession. "And all three of you are now set for this trip."

"I can't ask you to go with me," I said, turning from J.T. to Desmond.

"Don't be stupid, Ezri," Desmond scoffed. "We're safer with you than by ourselves and like your dad said, it's safer for us to be out of the country right now."

"What about your families?" I protested.

"After Shawna's attack, I told my parents to get out of town until I let them know it was safe to come back," J.T. answered.

"I've told Avery the same and they won't go after my dad. He doesn't have magic, remember? We've taken care of our families, Ez. Let us take care of you," Desmond added.

I didn't hate the idea of having the two most important men in my life with me along for this trip. I'd come to rely on them to get me out of sticky situations. Besides they were right, knowing they were with me made them safer, at least in the short term.

The plan was great in theory, but I couldn't just take off without advance notice to Captain Beech. Plus, I couldn't ask Jacquie to lie for me. I had no idea how long I'd be gone. I still needed to ensure the rest of the council remained safe in my absence. I might not be able to leave magical safeguards in place, but I could still leave some non-magical badasses to watch over them.

FOURTEEN

I walked into the diner and spotted Jacquie at a booth. A blonde woman sat across from my partner and I slid into the bench seat beside her. Special Agent Molly Cartwright had been an asset in rescuing Neveah and solving the kidnappings three months ago. She was still handling the news about magic better than I'd expected.

"What's the emergency?" Molly sipped from a half-empty mug.

"You didn't fill her in?" I addressed Jacquie.

"Your show, you tell it."

"The Order is attacking Council members, stealing the magic from their bloodlines. I have to go to Dublin to figure out how to stop them and maybe along the way find why my family line is so much more powerful than anyone else. We leave in ..." I checked my phone. "Four hours."

"Okay, first ... it's good to see you, too. You never write, you never call. I thought we had such a good thing going." Molly smiled and nudged my shoulder with hers. "But seriously, who is we?"

"Desmond and J.T."

"Your ... cousin and boyfriend. Got it. So, you need us to hold down the fort, I take it?"

"I've told everyone to stay inside, because the attacks have been happening in public places."

Jacquie slid a file across the table to Molly. "This is the guy behind it. He's got a rap sheet a mile long, but nothing has ever stuck."

"The bigger issue is, I don't have a leave request in, and Captain Beech is kind of a stickler for that sort of thing," I volunteered.

"I can cover you," Jacquie said.

"I can't ask you to do that. I don't know when I'll be back and one of us needs to stay in her good graces.'

"So, let me handle it then," Molly said, pushing the file back to Jacquie.

I eyed her warily. "What do you mean?"

"The FBI asks for loaner officers from local precincts all the time for special assignments. We just tell her you've been detailed to one effective immediately and that will cover you."

"Wait ... Don't you need paperwork for those kinds of things?" *Why was I fighting her on this? It was as good a plan as any.*

"You know how bureaucracy works. It will take weeks to get it all sorted out. And you let me worry about all that, okay? You need to do whatever you have to so you can beat these people at their own game. Jacquie and I will look after your people. If we get lucky and can nail this bastard on something while you're away, all the better."

"YOU CAN'T JUST WALK IN HERE and take one of my best Detectives," Captain Beech argued, slamming the door to her office closed behind her.

"With all due respect, Captain, that's the very reason we need her. I saw how Detective Trenton operated with that kidnapping case. She's good police and that is exactly what we need for this taskforce."

"I'm happy to do it, Captain," I chimed in, trying to sell the charade.

"And I'm sure I can handle flying solo for a little while," Jacquie added. "Besides, we all know this would look good on Ezri's record. Getting detailed to an FBI taskforce six months after earning her Detective's shield at her age. It's practically unheard of. It would show the brass how capable she is of protecting this city and its people."

Captain Beech held up a hand for silence. "I can

see I'm already outvoted. Do I at least get to know the nature of the taskforce?"

"Human trafficking ring," Molly blurted before I could stop her.

"Good luck to you on that one. Trenton, you're sure you are okay with doing this?"

"Yes, Captain. I haven't been more sure of anything in a long time. This is where I'm needed right now.'

"All right. Well, get out of my office and go save some lives."

I planned to do just that. I followed Jacquie and Molly out of the captain's office and back to the parking lot. "I texted Jacquie the list of council members who are still in the city. I need you to check on them every day. They know they should limit going out in public, but these people are stubborn. They have power, they know it, and they think that means they're invulnerable, despite them knowing that three of their own have been robbed of those same abilities."

"We'll set up rotating shifts," Molly said.

"In the mean time we'll keep monitoring the pawn shop. So far no one has showed," Jacquie added.

Her statement earned an eyebrow raise. "Wait ... I thought we didn't have anything to support putting people on the pawn shop."

"We don't, but I have a couple of friends who

owe me a favor. If we can find a way to take Wickham out of play with one of the necklaces on him, we will."

"And we just have to hope the magic within remains viable until I can get back to fix things."

"We've got this covered, Ezri. Get ready for your flight," Molly urged.

I nodded and left the two women standing in the parking lot. I didn't know what I needed to bring with me to Ireland, but something told me the genealogy was important. I also wanted to make sure Headquarters was as secure as it could be before I flew thousands of miles away.

When I arrived, there were no cars in the circular drive. Maybe news had spread through the rest of the community and families were staying away, keeping their children close. I wouldn't blame them if they had. We couldn't be sure this would stop with the Council. I stepped through the front door and nearly collided with a fast-moving blur of a boy.

"Sorry," he said, stepping back after bumping into me.

I looked down to see Lola Cox's little brother, Teddy. He remained in foster care, but at least he knew the truth about him and his sister's abilities. He didn't fully understand the extent of her involvement in the Order's dealings. Although he knew enough that I sometimes caught him sitting alone, because he worried that someday he would end up like her.

"You're good. Are you the only one here?" I replied.

"Yeah. Everyone else went home. I don't know why though. I didn't have anywhere else to go. My ride doesn't get here until late."

"I know I haven't had a chance to check in lately. But, how are you doing? Fitting in okay?" Objectively, I knew I didn't have time for this conversation. However in my heart, I knew I needed to ensure his well-being. I'd promised a dying Lola I'd look after him.

"I'm okay. I miss Lola. Sometimes I dream about her. I wonder if she knew the stuff I'm learning about."

"I'm sure she did. Hey, you want to help me do something extra special?"

His eyes lit up. "What?"

"I have to go away for a little while, but I wanted to make sure that this place is safe for everyone."

"You're going to do a spell. Can I watch?"

"Even better. I need your help to cast it."

He beamed at me. "What do I do?"

I led him out to the front steps and took his hand. "I want you to think about making this place invisible to people who aren't supposed to be here. Can you do that, Teddy?"

"Yeah. Then what?"

"Then, I want you to close your eyes and imagine a giant protective bubble around the whole building."

He nodded wordlessly and I caught a hint of thyme as his magic bloomed weakly beside me. I lent it the strength of my own power and watched as the magic raced along the walls, the windows, and into every crevice and crack, sealing in the good magic and keeping away the bad.

"Now it will be protected, and it will be even stronger when you're here," I said, patting his shoulder. I'd told Lola I would look after and protect him. Despite the Order's plans, for a little while, at least, he could still be safe.

SEPTEMBER 19, 2017

FIFTEEN

Aching pain in my neck woke me before the gentle jabs to my ribcage. I cracked one eyelid open and found a redheaded man with a neatly trimmed beard standing at the end of our row handing out forms. I tried to straighten up, but tendrils of agony shot down my spine. I realized that somehow I'd been sleeping in a position that had made the entire right side of my body go numb.

"Here you are Miss," the flight attendant said and passed three forms our way.

I awkwardly took them passing them to Desmond and J.T. who sat crammed in beside me.

"We should be landing soon," Desmond noted and started on the form.

I stared blankly at mine, my brain not quite caught up with the rest of me as pins and needles cascaded down my body. I let out a hint of magic to ease the transition and it buoyed me to fully alert.

"They want to know when we're leaving. We don't know the answer to that question," I hissed to Des.

"Put a week. Chances are, if we haven't found what we came here for by then, we're screwed anyways."

I scribbled down the same date as him, feeling almost like I was cheating on a test.

As soon as we landed, I intended to check in with Jacquie and Molly back home. If they could give me something positive, like they'd arrested Reuben on something like a traffic violation, I'd be happy. I knew he had other people doing his dirty work for him. Although having him off the street meant that he wasn't collecting the necklaces and maybe, just maybe, we could get back the rest of them and return what was stolen.

"So, while we were in New York, I looked online and found a cheap hotel not far from the airport," J.T. said, setting his already filled out customs form in the seat pocket in front of him.

"I don't know what I'd do without the two of you," I said and gave him a grateful look. I'd kiss him if Des wasn't wedged between us.

Desmond smiled at me. "Did you think you'd be saying those words six months ago when you walked into my office?' He'd apparently told the department he was putting in vacation time for an impromptu honeymoon.

"No, I didn't. I'm glad you proved me wrong."

The flight attendant returned to our row to review our forms. He flipped through them and my anxiety spiked as he studied each one in turn. I'd been exhausted by the time we'd made it to this leg of the trip and I'd fallen asleep not long after take-off. That much I remembered. Since we hadn't given anyone else the flight details, my brain was clearly panicking over nothing. Yet, I hadn't seen him examine anyone else's forms. My hands gripped the arm rests until my knuckles went white.

"What's wrong?" Desmond hissed in my ear.

"Does he look like he's overly interested in what we wrote?"

Desmond leaned forward to get a better look. By now, the flight attendant was handing them back, moving down several rows. "Not really. Why, are you getting a bad vibe?'

I rubbed my face. "I don't know. It's probably just stress and all the traveling. Maybe I'm just out of whack. I mean, for all we know the Order was watching all of us and they followed us to the airport."

"Ez, your dad said the flight was booked completely after we got our seats. So, even if they did figure out where we were going, they wouldn't beat us there. They certainly wouldn't be able to slip an operative on this exact plane either," Desmond said, using his reassuring therapist voice.

"I just can't shake that they know what we're doing and laughing at us. We've been a step behind them since the very start."

J.T. nudged Desmond in the arm and the two did the awkward dance of switching seats. With J.T. now by my side, I leaned against his shoulder. He squeezed my hand. "You have a right to worry that they're tracking us. It would make sense, but you took precautions before we left. You put the Council's safety and security in the hands of two extremely competent law enforcement agents."

"I know. I just need to know that no one else has been hit while we were away. That's all.'

"And once we land and get our phones figured out, we will do that. I promise."

"Tell me about the hotel," I said, needing the distraction.

"Just a single room, two beds. It will be cramped, but it will do until we figure out where we're headed."

I still didn't know where that was. I hadn't had time to try and interpret whatever the vision had been. As I settled against J.T. for the rest of the flight, I tried to figure out what I'd seen and how the magic had been able to do what it did, pulling me in from a single touch to the genealogy. I was certain other members of the family had touched it, too. Yet, none of their essences hinted at recognizing what I'd witnessed.

Intent fuels all magic, good or bad and the family pendant proved that intent could last even after the practitioner had passed away. But, why? *"Because the magic never truly dies,"* Theodora's voice whispered in my head. Whoever had created the genealogy clearly imbued it with power and the intention had been to map the family tree all the way from the very beginning of our line. Meaning that my ancestor whose name I couldn't pronounce had put that intent out into the world hundreds of years ago and somehow, it had endured all this time. Maybe because our bloodline had lasted for so long or maybe because their magic was just that powerful. And yet, we'd never questioned why ours had so much more oomph compared to other people, until now. Why?

That still didn't give us a starting point. Even so maybe a little guided trip down memory lane would get us there. I knew there was more of a technique to it than what I'd done on myself and others. The way Desmond guided people through their own traumas was a skill I didn't possess, even with my Savior status.

"When we get to the hotel, I'm going to need your help to see what I can piece together from that vision," I said, making eye contact with Desmond.

"Whatever you need." I could see the worry lines

creasing his forehead. Despite the brave face he was putting on, I knew he was worried for his family.

MY STOMACH RUMBLED with hunger as I stepped up to the Customs counter and handed over my ID, passport, and the form I'd filled out on the plane. The officer—a middle-aged man with salt and pepper hair and half-moon glasses—looked at me with a neutral expression.

"Purpose for coming to Dublin, Ma'am," he asked in clipped English.

"Pleasure. Doing some family genealogy," I replied.

"Hope you find what you're looking for. Have a good visit," he said and handed back my passport and ID.

"Thanks." I followed the winding ropes leading out of the customs area and into the airport proper. Desmond and J.T. waited for me, both fiddling with their phones.

"Give me your phone. I think I figured it out," J.T. said and held his hand out toward me.

I passed it over and watched him fiddle with the settings. Desmond's lips pressed into a thin line, the rest of his expression unreadable as he stared at a message on his phone.

"What is it?" Part of me didn't want to know.

"Avery just checking in. She may have hacked our travel itinerary to make sure we landed okay."

"As much as I like your wife and her amazing tech skills, if she could hack it that easy, people who we don't want to have our information could do the same," I reminded him.

"I know. But this is Avery. She's smart and knows how to cover her tracks."

J.T. handed my phone back to me. I saw I had a missed call from Jacquie and a couple texts from Dad. I hit the play button on Jacquie's message and pressed it to my ear as we walked toward baggage claim.

"Hey partner, just hoping you're settling into that assignment okay. Things are fine here, nothing new although our friend stopped by to pick up that present, we thought about getting. Guess we'll have to find another one. Call when you're able."

"Shit," I muttered, drawing my traveling companions' attention. "Reuben got his hands on the third necklace. But so far, she doesn't think anyone else has been attacked."

"That's something at least," J.T. offered, wrapping an arm around my waist.

"Hey, we'll grab the bags. Why don't you figure out how we get a cab?" Desmond said, leading J.T. away toward a carousel full of suitcases in various shapes and shades of black and grey.

I checked the texts from Dad. He'd sent a couple

of images taken of pages from mom's books. They were close ups, but I couldn't read them without enlarging them. An ocean away and he was still trying to help. There was a single text message beneath the pictures. 'Mom had contact with a man named Iain Nobles not long before she died. See above for contact.' I scrolled back up to see that this Iain guy lived in Dublin.

"How's that cab coming?" Desmond asked, returning with our luggage.

"Haven't gotten there yet. But I think we have our next step," I said showing him the images and Dad's message.

"See, and you were worried we'd be aimlessly traipsing around a foreign country," Desmond said, eyeing J.T. with a smirk.

I wanted to take in the hustle and bustle of the city as we sat crammed in the back of a small cab weaving through traffic. Except that I couldn't stop thinking about the fact that Mom had been looking into our family history a decade ago. Who was this Iain Nobles and what did he know about magic? Lack of Wi-Fi meant I couldn't do a quick search for him while we sat in traffic.

"So, what are you all doing here in Dublin?" The cabbie asked.

"Just visiting. Looking to find out if we have any family roots in the area," Desmond said. Another version of the truth. Easier to keep track of the lies and half-truths when they weren't completely made up.

"We've definitely got some great libraries in the city and historical records."

"Thanks. We'll be sure to check them out," I said, fidgeting with my phone case as he pulled up to the small hotel J.T. had booked.

"Well, they're mighty friendly, so don't be shy," he chatted on as J.T. handed over payment and we climbed out. He must have done a currency exchange while I was still in the Customs line.

"A local historical society might not be a bad idea," J.T. suggested as we stepped into the chilly lobby.

"We have a point of contact. First we need to see who this guy is and why Mom thought he could be useful. Remember, we're on borrowed time," I snapped, regretting my tone immediately. "Sorry, I didn't mean to get all cranky I'm just tired, hungry, and my body doesn't know what day it is."

"I forgot you haven't traveled much," Desmond said, patting my back and stepping up to the counter.

I lingered by the front door, studying the cars and people as they passed by on the street. It all looked normal, but felt much older. I let the sandalwood charm do its thing and wash away the scent of my own magic from the plane ride. Breathing deeply I concentrated and closed my eyes to let my other senses take over.

The air grew heavier as the magic in the world here bumped up against my skin, wrapping around me like a cat greeting a new person and claiming it as its own. It wasn't an unpleasant feeling. It almost felt like the magic was welcoming me home, even though I'd never been here before. Even though all signs pointed to my family's magic originating from here so in a way, I was coming home. A host of scents wafted toward me as a door opened but I couldn't identify all of them, my frame of reference was suddenly too small.

"I always longed to visit the land of our forefathers," Theodora said beside me.

"It's a pretty sight, I'll give you that," Grandma said from the other side.

"What do you know about a man named Iain Nobles," I whispered, addressing my grandmother.

"Never heard of him," she said with a shrug. "But if your mother was looking to contact him, then I'd say you're on the right track. Still, you need to be careful. You're not on your home turf anymore, Ezzie."

"I know. But it feels like I belong here," I murmured.

"You ready to get some rest?" J.T. said, stepping up behind me and kissing my ear.

"Yeah," I said as Grandma and Theodora faded back into the pendant. They'd be there when I needed them again.

SIXTEEN

Food and a nap refreshed both my body and my mood. I sat up and looked around the small room. J.T. slept soundly on the bed beside me. Desmond sat at the tiny desk shoved in the far corner beneath one of the two exterior windows, pouring over the genealogy.

"Find anything new?" I asked and hovered over his left shoulder.

"No. Yet, even I can feel the magic in this. It's ancient. Older than anything I've ever experienced, but I don't see anything when I touch it, even though we're both descended from the same ancestors." He traced his family line back up to Eleanor Pruitt.

"I think maybe the message, or whatever it is, was meant specifically for me," I said.

Des nodded, a somber look on his face. "That's

what I figured too. I just hoped that for once, being a part of this bloodline would give me something extra."

"You have helped me do so many things, Des. If you hadn't come back into my life when you did, I couldn't have stopped the Order from raising those demons or rescued the girls. You may not be the Savior, but you're damn well mine."

"I appreciate the vote of confidence, but sometimes I feel jealous of you having this epic destiny."

"Trust me, it's not all it's cracked up to be. The chance of dying is like a million times higher and you don't want that many people hating you," I told him with a soft laugh.

"You're right. So, while you were recovering, I did a little digging on our mystery man Iain Nobles."

"Please tell me he's still alive," I muttered.

Desmond pulled out his laptop and turned it so I could read the entry on the screen. A man with just a touch of gray in his jet-black hair stared back at me. Professor Iain Nobles taught metaphysics at a nearby university.

"Definitely not dead," I said, feeling just a little guilty about the rush of hormones flooding my body at the sight of the handsome man while my equally attractive boyfriend lay in bed near me.

"It lists office hours for lunch time. We could pay him a visit and see what he knows," Des suggested.

"We don't even know if he's magical," I pointed out.

Des tapped the side of his nose. "It's too bad we don't know someone with the ability to pick up on magical signatures."

"Asshole!" I said and slapped his arm. "I should check in with Dad again and make sure he's doing okay."

"You do that and I'll get J.T.'s butt out of bed," Desmond said.

"Let him sleep. No need for all three of us to go running around a city we don't know chasing ghosts and maybes."

"I'll be ready to go in ten," he said and disappeared into the tiny bathroom.

After double checking that international calling was active on my phone, I dialed Dad's number. I tried to calculate the time difference in my head as the phone rang and realized too late that it was really early in the morning back home.

On the fifth ring, Dad's voice came through groggily. "Hello?"

"Dad, sorry, I forgot what time it was there," I said.

"It's fine. Are you okay? Did you get my messages?"

"I did.. We're on our way to meet with the professor now. Thanks for still looking for answers."

"Of course. I'm glad you got there safe."

"Hey, Dad, you haven't noticed anyone hanging around the house lately have you?" I assumed it was common knowledge that my mother was the magical one in the family. Despite that it was still possible that the Order had the rest of my family under surveillance.

"Not that I noticed But, let them follow me around. They'll get bored really fast. Unless they like bowling," he said through a yawn.

"Stay safe, Dad. I'll let you know what we find."

"I love you," he replied.

"Love you, too." I ended the call just as Desmond reappeared in a fresh shirt and he'd clearly combed his hair. He was checking his pockets for the hotel key, his phone, and wallet. I did the same, slinging a bag I'd picked up at the airport over my shoulder with the genealogy inside and scribbled a quick note for J.T. on the pad by the phone.

"Let's go see a professor about some metaphysics," Desmond said brightly.

THE ANCIENT SENSE of power permeated the city as we walked, taking in the beautiful architecture. Des and I passed tiny shops and pubs shuttered until evening as we sat side by side on a bus that supposedly would take us to the university.

"Can you feel it? The depth of magic here," I

asked in a hushed tone as the bus eased to a halt at a stop sign.

"It's incredible," Desmond agreed, leaning past me to look out the window. "I thought Boston was old and powerful but this ... this is an entirely different level."

"But it feels right, like we're meant to be here," I said, settling back against the bus seat.

"Have you had any more visions of where we're supposed to go?"

"Not since before we left home. I've been trying to think about what I saw, slow it down. Though I'm going to need your help. And even if we could figure out what it means or where its leading us, having a local to act as a guide wouldn't be a bad thing."

"How much do we even know about Professor Nobles? Did your mother even make contact?"

I shook my head. "I don't know. Dad didn't say." I pulled my phone from my pocket and looked at the images he'd sent again. They were definitely images of printed emails, but they only looked to be sent to Professor Nobles. Nothing referring to replies back. Bringing up old correspondence from a decade ago was a long shot, but we had to follow every lead that came our way.

"Oy, Miss, this is you," the driver said, waving his hand to get our attention.

The bus eased to a stop, Desmond and I climbed off. The building was imposing in a much more obvious way than the Authority headquarters. I chalked it up to the fact that everything in this city was far older than the city of Boston. Now we just had to find Professor Nobles and hope he wasn't too busy to answer some very weird questions from American 'tourists'.

SEVENTEEN

We spent a good twenty minutes wandering around the campus until a student took pity on us and pointed us in the right direction. The door to Professor Nobles' office sat ajar as we approached.

"Have you figured out how you're going to introduce yourself yet?" Des whispered in my ear as I raised my hand to knock.

My mouth went dry and I stopped mid-motion. He wouldn't care that I was a police detective from another country's jurisdiction. Besides for all we knew, he didn't know anything about magic so introducing myself as the Savior seemed a bit much, too. I didn't have time to formulate an answer before the door swung inward and a force collided with me.

"Oomph," I groaned and staggered backwards, falling against Desmond's arm.

"Oh, so sorry," the owner of the body who'd

slammed into me absently apologized. The man looked up from a cell phone and his gaze narrowed. "Have we met?"

"No, but you're Professor Iain Nobles," I replied and steadied my balance. He looked exactly like his picture and that rush of attraction hit me again.

"I am. And who exactly are you?"

"My name is Ezri Trenton," I began, desperately searching for the best descriptor for why I mattered to this total stranger.

"Wait ... like the prophesied to stop evil forces Ezri Trenton?"

I gaped at him, words utterly failing me. Beside me, out of the corner of my eye, I caught Desmond staring at him open-mouthed, too. "Um ... yes, but how do you ..."

"It's quite the long story." He checked his phone again. "I'm sorry. I'm guessing you've come a long way, but I'm late for a lecture. You're welcome to stay here until I get back in an hour. I'll have some food sent up if you like."

"Sure, thanks." The words left my mouth before I could be angry that we'd found our guy, but upon meeting he was bailing on us.

"Wonderful." He grinned. "Can't believe I've actually met you." His tone was that of a fan boy in awe. There were so many questions whirling in my head competing for my attention. Like how did he know about me? Moreover, why was he so eager to meet me?

I led the way into Professor Nobles' office to find a warmly decorated space that reminded me a little of Desmond's office at the precinct. There were bookshelves filled with thick-spined books in various states of disrepair. As I settled into the rolling chair behind the desk, I picked up the scent of something heady, like a spice I couldn't quite remember the name of.

"Do you smell that?" I looked to Desmond.

"All I smell are old books," he replied and leaned on the desk. "You getting something less mundane?"

"Maybe." I spun around in the chair. "So, you think he'd mind if we did a little memory deconstruction while we wait?"

"What he doesn't know won't hurt him," Desmond answered and pulled one of the other chairs around to sit beside me.

"I'm glad you're here with me," I said and took both of his hands in mine.

"We're family, Ez. This is what we do. Now, close your eyes and let me guide you."

I let the cooling scent of spearmint wash over me. Unlike the first time we'd tried this exercise after I'd been stabbed, my magic didn't rise up to meet his. It knew now that his magic meant no harm. Submitting easily, I sunk back into the memory of being in my living room and following the family tree to the roots.

"I'm there," I murmured.

"Tell me what you see," he prompted, his voice miles away and yet I felt his presence right beside me as I studied the genealogy.

"I'm looking at the genealogy. I'm at the top. I really wish I could pronounce this name." *Aoife.*

"I'm sure our new friend can help you translate or sort it out. Have you been hit with the vision yet?"

"No, not yet." I watched as Memory Me went into a trance, clearly experiencing the vision I'd been hit with. "Okay, it's happening. I'm going to try to slow it down and make it bigger," I said.

My magic filled the space in my mind. Then the wall became a screen showing a slideshow of all of the images from the vision. I stepped close, finally able to control the speed at which they passed by. There was the figure in the cave, but maybe it wasn't a cave now that I looked closer. It was dark, but there were different levels of shadow around the figure. I tried to reach out to feel what was in the vision, to extend my senses further, but all I got was static. Whoever, or whatever, had sent the vision didn't want me getting that close, at least not yet. The figure vanished, replaced by bright sunlight with a flurry of color and noise.

"Can you give me a little signal boost, Des. I think I see something." Spearmint tickled the back of my nose and the image went still.

Hundreds of people in modern, colorful outfits

stood around what looked like a large rock formation and I tried to commit the scene to memory before letting the rest of the vision play out. We passed the sign for the Dublin airport and I caught yet another whiff of that spice. That hadn't been there when the vision hit the first time.

I pushed myself out of the memory, bumping up against Desmond's magic holding me inside. I squeezed my cousin's hands and the intensity of his magic evaporated. I opened my eyes to find Professor Nobles standing in the doorway, looking awestruck. His dark brown eyes were wide, and his mouth hung open like he was about to comment on how crazy we looked, sitting in his office holding hands.

"Sorry, this is just fascinating," he finally said and pulled the door shut behind him.

"Not to sound rude, but what exactly did you see?" For the first time, I was self-conscious about using my magic. I didn't know how much this man knew or had witnessed.

"What looked to be guided meditation, but I have a suspicion there was more to it than that."

Time to find out what this man really knew. "How do you know who I am?"

"You're practically famous," he raved, settling into the other chair on the opposite side of his desk.

"No, I'm not. How do you know about what I was … supposed to do?"

"Supposed to do?" His dark brows inched up his forehead. "You mean you've done it already?"

"Six months ago. It may have escaped your notice over here, but we had a pretty big eclipse and a meteor shower on the Equinox.'

"Oh, believe me, I felt it. I think we all did. We were sorting out our energies for weeks after. However, that was just an accidental confluence of celestial phenomena."

"Maybe, but some very bad people took advantage of it," Desmond interjected.

"I suppose they would. And you're sure the terms have been met? I mean, I know she never shared the exact specifics with me, but I didn't think it would have been that soon."

Enough beating around the bush. "You know what magic is, don't you?"

The bemused wonder and awe at my presence vanished, replaced by hard lines and a serious brow furrow. "Of course, I know about magic. What do you think we've just been talking about? The bloody weather?"

"So, you knew my mother?" I prompted.

He nodded, that same spice scent wafting toward me. "She reached out with questions and we struck up a bit of a correspondence. She'd sent me a photo or two. You look like her."

I couldn't tell if there was supposed to be more to his comment than a simple compliment. Maybe my instincts as a detective had taught me to distrust people—criminals often used compliments to hide their real motives—kicked in. "What did you and my mother talk about?"

"She wanted to know if there were any ancient ties to magic here that she might use to protect you. I pointed her to a few rituals that could shield your presence, but then I never heard back from her on if they had worked or not."

A seed of dread settled in the pit of my stomach. "Did any of those rituals involve self-sacrifice?"

"One. It was the most powerful of the suggestions, but obviously the most dangerous."

I let out a bitter laugh. "Well, guess which one she picked."

"I'm so sorry, love. That ... she was trying to protect you from what was on the horizon. Like I said, she didn't give me specifics in so many words, but I knew a great destiny awaited her daughter."

"I know that. And I've made peace with that part of my past ... Finally. It took a really long time, but I have. Now, I need to focus on my future. There's another prophecy looming over me and I have no idea how I'm supposed to stop it. And the bastards who are the reason my mother is dead are stealing magic from members of our Council. I need to find out how to stop it."

"Sounds like you've got quite the dilemma on your hands. And you came to me because ..."

"Because her mother had your information and frankly, we didn't know where else to start," Desmond answered, his tone harsher than I thought the situation called for. Maybe bringing up my mother's death brought up bad memories for him, too.

Then again, why was I so at ease with this man, even if all he'd told me was that he's the reason my mother died. That he'd given her the playbook to operate from without really warning her about the consequences that would leave a fifteen-year-old behind. That spicy scent hit me again and suddenly I realized what was happening. He was using his own power to manipulate my emotions and reactions. I looked at him and my hormones flared again. *Is he using a glamour?*

I put out a little of my own will into the world to feel out the edges of his magic. It circled the room, like he'd built a little nest of magical security within the walls. Maybe we'd bumped up against it during our memory walk and it had decided it didn't like us being in its space. Or maybe he was trying to control me for some other reason. Either way, I wasn't going to let him win. I concentrated and found the usually invisible web of magic that exists in the world around us, following it back to him. One end of it coiled around my wrist, the other draped over him like a cloak. With a sharp flick of my hand, the bond broke and Professor Nobles slumped back in his chair. His air of attractiveness faded with the spell.

"I don't know what game you think you're play-ing, but don't you ever try to use magic to screw with my head," I snapped, launching to my feet.

"My apologies. I meant no disrespect. Once you mentioned your mother had taken the more lethal option, I worried I might have upset you and wanted to ensure there weren't any … tantrums. I don't make much and I can't afford to have this place fixed up should someone's temper flare."

"And the whole 'sexy silver fox' routine?"

He swallowed. "Just a bit of fun with the students is all. Nothing unwanted or illegal. You have my word."

Desmond cleared his throat and nodded toward the hallway. Whatever he needed to share couldn't be done in front of our host. Once we'd left the office behind, Desmond whispered, "How do we know he's not part of the Order?"

The thought had occurred to me, but I'd assumed that like the Authority, the Order's origins came out of the Witch Trials. However, maybe I'd been wrong. Theodora's journals clearly pointed to the origins of our family's magic being here in Ireland. From what little I knew of magical lore here, druids were the predominant wielders of magic during ancient times. "I'll check him out, but I feel like he was telling the truth just now."

"He was in your head, Ez. Hell, he still could be

right now. And if he suspects that *we* suspect him, he could be concealing the mark."

"I got this. Give me a minute or two in there alone." I held up a hand to quell any protest. "I need to cleanse the room and I can't have your magic muddling things up."

"I don't like it, but fine," he replied and stayed put when I went back into the office.

Professor Nobles hadn't moved from his seat. "Before we go any deeper into what brought us here, I need to know I can trust you. Having you poke around in my head and try to convince me of things doesn't exactly show that I can."

"Again, I was trying to ease pain. You have my word it will not happen again."

I sat down in his chair. "The thing is, as you can understand, I don't trust easily. So, the word of a man I just met doesn't mean a whole hell of a lot to me."

He nodded. "Yes, I can see that. Please, let me prove to you that I just want to help."

"Roll up your sleeves," I said and gestured to his forearms.

"Sorry?"

"I need to make sure you're not branded by the Order's mark. And just so you know, if you're using magic to conceal it, I'll be able to tell."

"I swear I'm not concealing anything."

"Just do it," I said, a wave of irritation and

exhaustion suddenly washing over me, sharpening my tone.

He had at least three decades on me, but he flinched at my words and rolled up his shirtsleeves. No scythe and triple spiral marred his skin on either arm. I stood and rounded the desk to peer at his neck. Nothing appeared there and I didn't feel any magic wrapping itself around him, not like before.

"You're clear," I said loudly hoping Desmond heard me.

"Tell me, how did you end up here in Ireland?" Nobles asked as Desmond returned and claimed the chair he'd been in before.

"Chasing our family lineage," I answered. My foot brushed the bag with the genealogy inside. He may not be an Order member, but I wasn't ready to let him see private family documents.

"I see." He rubbed his stubbled chin in silence for a few minutes. "You also said something about stolen magic?"

"The Order of Samael, basically the bane of my existence, is taking magic from our Council members and it's eliminating entire bloodlines. I haven't been able to recreate how they're doing it and still have no idea why they're taking it either."

"We really aren't sure you can even help us," Desmond chimed in.

Nobles let out a deep belly laugh. "Oh lad, you

think that just because I teach metaphysics I'm too much a scientist to solve your magic problem?"

"Maybe," Des replied.

"I teach it so that those who don't have the blessing of our gift might seek to understand how it could be possible to exist. So that when they inevitably encounter it, they're inclined to believe what they see, rather than dismiss it."

"Great, so you can help," I said before Desmond could say more.

"Aye. You said they've been eliminating entire bloodlines. That takes a great deal of skill."

"They're resourceful assholes," I answered.

"Tell me, is there a pattern to their targets?"

"They're taking the younger magic first. The families who joined the council more recently. From what we've been able to gather, their magic isn't as strong as Desmond's or mine. Our families have been on the Council since its inception in the early 1700s."

"And you say you don't know what they're doing with it?"

"We know they're collecting it in physical items, but after that, your guess is as good as mine. I'm thousands of miles away right now, so I know I can't stop them if they strike again. But, if I can get my hands on what's been stolen, is there a ritual that can return the magic to its rightful owners?"

"Love, there are rituals for everything, you just

need to know where to look." He stood from his chair and retreated to the bookshelf across the room.

I watched him browse the spines with a tender touch until he found the particular one he was looking for. "Now, I'm not keen on lending out my books to people, especially those I don't know well, but given your status in the community, I'll allow it."

He set the book down on the desk between us and I studied the faded text on the pressed leather. I put a hand on the front cover, expecting to be hit with another vision or at least a jolt of magic like I'd felt when we arrived in the country, but nothing happened. My face must have telegraphed disappointment, because Nobles snickered.

"It's just a book, lass. A history of magic in the region. A sort of catalog of how magic was used and the clashes of the locals going back centuries. You have your Council and this Order; well that struggle isn't new. It's been raging for long before your bloodline even began."

"Speaking of blood, I've been told the answer to my problem might lay in my bloodline," I said, reaching into the bag and pulling out the genealogy. If he was trusting me with something of great value to him, I could show a little in return. "We traced it all the way back here."

Nobles studied the page and ran a finger from my name at the bottom of the page all the way back to Aoife at the top. His lips moved but no words or sound came out, as if he were reading to himself or trying to figure out how to say something. "This can't be the same Aoife," he finally said aloud. The name flew out of his mouth so fast and in such a low tone I couldn't catch the way he pronounced it.

"I'm going to need more than that," I said.

He pulled the book back toward him, setting aside the genealogy. Focusing entirely on the book he flipped through the pages, passing spots and going back until he found whatever he needed to show us. Flipping the book around so I could read, he said, "Long ago, there were two rival sects of Druids. One light, one dark."

"That sounds familiar," Desmond offered softly.

I studied the text on the page.

As the time of great power approached, the leader of the protectors, Aoife, vowed that never again would the darkness rule this place or any other. She swore an oath to her sect and to the world that she would not rest until the darkness had been vanquished from this world for good.

"I mean, for all we know, this is a really common name," I said, sliding the book over so that Desmond could read the passage.

"Not that common, certainly not seven or eight hundred years ago," Nobles replied.

"Okay, so say that this person is the same as our ancestor, so what?"

He pointed to the genealogy. "There's nothing

that says this leads to here in Ireland, let alone Dublin. So, I'd be interested to know what specifically led you to my door?"

"My dad found my mother's emails to you in some of her belongings," I said, remaining intentionally vague.

"Did you know that information before you hopped a flight here?"

"No." The word leapt off my tongue before I could consider continuing the lie. I didn't sense any of his magic pulling the answer from me, but that didn't mean he wasn't trying to influence me.

"I've been truthful with you, let's stop playing games. If your people are losing their magic, it's for a purpose. I'm guessing you want to get back home as soon as you can to put a stop to it."

"I had a vision," I finally answered.

"A vision? That a common occurrence for your family?'

"Not exactly. Only one member of the family had the power of premonition and she belonged to Desmond's branch, not mine. Anyway, it wasn't like seeing the future or anything. It felt more like something from the past pulling me here. There was a lone figure and people in a big group. Then I saw the Dublin airport sign. That's it."

"I see. How about this, you take that book, get to know your history here, and I'll see what I can find for you. That sound like a fair deal? And if I do find anything, I'll take you there myself. As a way to make up for how we met."

A sharp knock on the door interrupted the conversation as a woman appeared carrying two paper bags. Professor Nobles gestured for her to leave them on the desk and she retreated.

"I promised you food and drink. Feel free to bring it along with you."

"Thanks, but how are you going to get in touch if you do find something? It's not like I have an international number."

"I'll find you." He tapped the side of his head. "I've a knack for recognizing the feel of a person's power and I've committed yours to memory. Some of the strongest I've ever encountered. I'll know where to find you."

His tone was a clear dismissal. So, I closed the book, retrieved the genealogy and placed both back in my bag. Desmond led the way out of the office and back to the entrance to campus.

"How are you holding up?" He asked when we reached the bus that would take us back to the hotel.

"I knew that my mom had to get the idea from somewhere. I just never thought it would be from a practitioner an ocean away." I shifted the weight of my bag to the other shoulder. "My gut says he's going to come through. I know he pushed us with his magic, and the glamour was a bit skeevy, but you heard him, I'm stronger than him. I don't think he could lie to me even if he wanted to."

"Any more visits from dead relatives?" He prodded as we boarded the bus and found seats near the back.

"Not since we left the hotel. Recently Grandma's been popping up more. I'd forgotten how sassy she could be."

"You didn't think you inherited that attitude from your parents, did you?" Desmond laughed. "That skipped a generation for sure.'

"I wish I could share this with you. I wish you could have met Eleanor. I know it was only a part of her, but she was kind. She reminded me of you."

"I guess some traits are enduring in families across generations, no matter how far back you go."

Which made me wonder if Iain was right and the Aoife from his book was the same who sat at the base of our family tree. If she was, then what did that mean for the prophecy currently hanging over my head and the Order's plans for their pilfered magic?

Time's quickly running out to slot all the pieces of the puzzle together and we still didn't even know what the damn picture was supposed to look like.

EIGHTEEN

We got back to the hotel to find J.T. stepping out of the bathroom. He looked well rested, at least that made one of us. He tugged on a clean shirt and pulled me in for a quick kiss.

"So, what did I miss on your city-spanning adventure?"

"We found Iain Nobles. He's a practitioner like us," I began, settling on the edge of the bed closest to the window.

"He gave Ezri's mother the spell that she used ..." Desmond trailed off.

"Oh ... oh shit. Ez, I'm so sorry." J.T. sat beside me and took my hand in his. "Please tell me you didn't send him flying."

"I didn't. I'm okay, really. He is doing some digging to help with the vision I had and he gave us some more information to look into." I pulled out the book. "There were two ancient sects of Druids back in the day and a woman who has the same name as our ancestor led the light practitioners."

J.T. squeezed my hand. "And you think that's the key to figuring out how to stop the Order's plans?"

"Maybe. There was a passage in here about how this woman vowed to fight until darkness was wiped from the earth and to protect people. I need to find out everything I can about her."

"Immersing yourself in this place's history is a start," Theodora said, appearing by the desk across the room.

I needed to get out of the hotel and let the city's magic guide me to wherever I was meant to go. I'd spend time with the book, but I needed to do it somewhere other than a tiny hotel room with two hovering, if well-meaning, bodyguards. It would get too confusing conversing with dead relatives only I could see while having to relay the other half of the conversation to them.

"I'm going for a walk. Maybe some fresh air will help this all make more sense," I announced and slung the bag back over my shoulder.

"But, isn't it safer to stay out of sight? We don't know how far the Order reaches or what other trouble might be out there," J.T. protested.

"He's right. There's too much unknown, Ezri. We all agree, you are powerful. However, you are still human and that means you can be hurt," Desmond added.

"Just because Iain knew who I was, who I *really* am, doesn't mean everyone does. Just like back home, not every person with magic knows my face. I'll be fine, guys. I just need a little space."

Theodora appeared beside me in the hallway and as I eased the door shut, I heard Desmond say, "I'll bet you twenty bucks her Grandma just showed up and she doesn't want us to hear the conversation."

He may have guessed the wrong relative, but his sentiment wasn't wrong. It wasn't that I didn't want them to hear the conversation. It was more I wasn't in the mood to translate half of the conversation. As a precaution I stuck in Bluetooth headphones so at least to the outside observer, it would look like I was having a conversation on the phone rather than talking to myself.

"Who would have thought you'd be learning about history to save the world?" Grandma popped up on my other side as soon as I left the hotel lobby.

"So, you're just going to tag-team me now?" I asked and started wandering, not sure where I would end up.

"We are here to aid you," Theodora said.

"It would be more helpful if you could tell me what the Order is planning to do with the stolen magic. Or what the new prophecy means so I can stop it from happening."

"Premonitions of what is to come are meant for shaping actions, not to be prevented."

"Well, I definitely prevented the bad guys from winning last time," I replied.

"But you didn't know how that was going to happen until you were in the thick of it. You can prepare all you want, but so many things go into making a situation what it is," Grandma added.

"Though I won't know how to fight what's coming if I don't know what that something is."

I stopped walking and turned toward a display in a jewelry shop. Pentacles of varying sizes—some with different gemstones at their center, hung in the window. Before I realized what was happening, I had stepped inside. A slender woman with gray hair sat behind the counter.

"Hello, dear," she greeted with a thick accent.

"Hi." I stepped up to the counter.

"Looking for something in particular as a memento?"

"Sorry?"

She leaned forward and gave me a smile. "You're not from these parts. You looking for something to remember your trip by?"

"No, I was wondering if you could tell me how old a particular piece of jewelry is?" Undoing the clasp around my neck, I laid the pentacle on the glass countertop between us.

The woman picked up the necklace and studied

it under a bright light. "I'm not an expert mind you, but I would say this is old. Very old indeed. I don't have anything close to it's likeness here."

"Would you say maybe seven or eight hundred years old?" I probed.

"Could be. If it is, I'm surprised it's lasted this long. You've kept it in remarkable condition. What makes you think it has that lengthy a history?"

"Family stories," I answered and in a way, it was true. I didn't know how else to explain the feelings I got when I'd touched the genealogy. It was like older magic had touched the pendant, but not in the same way as my family had since the Witch Trials.

"If you're right and it is that old, I'm quite surprised to see a diamond. They were quite rare in these parts back then. I'd say you aren't in need of anything from my shop. More likely you need a proper appraiser."

"Oh, I'm not trying to sell it. I just wanted confirmation on if it really could be that old," I said, extending a hand to take it back.

She relinquished it, but continued to eye me. "There's something about you, I can tell. Something about your aura tells me you carry a lot on your shoulders, and this is just one more weight on you."

I redid the clasp and as the metal brushed the skin of my collarbone, the tiny shop vanished, replaced by the darkness of night and the same figure I'd seen before in my vision. Except this time, the figure turned to reveal a woman with dark red hair and pale skin. Her eyes were seafoam green and around her neck hung a pentacle without any stone at its heart. Even though I knew it was a vision, I reached to my own throat to feel the weight of the pendant around my neck. In her hands, the woman held something small and brilliant. The diamond that would come to be at the heart of my pendant?

"Seek me, blood of my blood. I await you," a disembodied voice called.

"Love, you all right?" The shop owner's voice disrupted the vision before I could call out or ask any more questions.

"Yeah, sorry. Uh, thanks for your help." I raced from the shop and down a nearby alley, pressing my back to cool stone as I willed my heart to beat slower. My right hand clamped down hard on the pendant and strawberries bloomed all around me, begging the world to take me back there. If I had just another minute, I could sort this all out.

"I need to see," I whispered and felt hot tears dampening my cheeks.

"The gift of foresight and vision does not work that way," Theodora said softly taking my free hand in hers. "That is how Eleanor explained. It came when the world needed it. Not when she wished to know what was to come."

"But whatever I'm seeing has to be in the past. Really far back if we're right about this ancient sect of druids. I'm not trying to see something that hasn't happened yet."

"I would believe the same rules apply in this instance. You may wish to know all there is about our foremother, but perhaps it is she who is not yet ready to share it with you."

A complaint about the fact this woman was long dead soured on my tongue. Theodora had died centuries ago, too. Yet she'd been helpful at times and here she stood. "Say you're right and these things happen when the world needs to know them, clearly the Order is planning something, and we still have that other prophecy to untangle. Right about now sounds like a great time for the world to need to know this information."

"Was this vision the same as before?"

I settled the Bluetooth headphone back in my ear and started walking back the way I'd come. "No. She turned around and had the pentacle around her neck." My thumb brushed against the tiny stone. "It looked like mine, but without the stone. She said she was waiting for me and I'm supposed to seek her out."

"And you are doing as she asks now. You are using every avenue presented to you to seek her," Theodora said.

What if it's not enough? "For the first time in a long time, I feel like magic is just jerking me around. It wants me to stop the bad guys. Fine, I can do that.

It's my job. But I am not all-knowing. It could give me a bigger hint than visions played out in ten second clips. I've done what magic has asked of me countless times. I feel like it's punishing me or testing me and that's not fair."

"Life isn't fair, sweetheart," Grandma popped up on my other side. "Never has been truth be told. If it were, we'd all be a big happy commune of witches living it up. You haven't been given anything you can't handle."

I snorted. "That's easy for you to say. You don't have to fight the torture-happy, kidnapping maniacs."

"Do not forget, we are a part of you. Your struggles and triumphs become ours," Theodora interjected.

"But people aren't looking to you to put everything back together when shit hits the fan."

"What's this really about, Ezzie? You haven't been so doom and gloom before. And you've been behind the eight ball plenty," Grandma noted, wrapping a translucent arm around my shoulders.

I could almost feel the weight of her body pressed against mine. Theodora took my hand and gave it a squeeze. "Your grandmother observes rightly. I do not believe that you fear the Order targeting innocents as a way to harm you. They have employed such means before."

I stopped walking and closed my eyes, steadying myself. "Because for the first time, what if I really am alone to face them? They're attacking the council, the people who are supposed to have my back. I can't rely on them if they don't have magic to use."

"You're never alone, honey," Grandma said, giving me a 'don't be stupid' look.

"But, I kind of am. Sure, I can call on your magic but once it's used up, you're gone forever, and I can feel the power in the pentacle dwindling. I can't risk burning through that surplus of magic when I don't know where or how I'd ever replace it."

Grandma moved to bar my path. Even though I was pretty sure I could walk through her with no problem, I stayed put. She crossed her arms over her chest and shook her head.

"Stop that right now. You're feeling sorry for yourself and I won't stand for it. And neither would your mother. We raised you to be strong, Ezri. I refuse to believe you being the one to fulfill Eleanor's prophecy was a random chance of genes. The world was waiting for you. You did miraculous things and you're going to do them again, because you have the power to do them."

I blinked at her tirade, grateful no one else could hear her words. I probably looked like a dumbstruck tourist taking up far too much space on the sidewalk as I let her words sink in. In her own gruff way, Grandma was telling me she believed in me and my ability to overcome the odds. She was right. I could do this. I'd made it this far, which is probably more than the Order expected. Yes, I'd left the Council with less protection than if I'd stayed, but something told me they weren't worrying about my part of the prophecy. Whatever plans they were hatching were probably an attempt to fulfill their part of it.

"You're right. I've got this." The weight of Iain's borrowed book suddenly felt like a fifty-pound dumbbell on my shoulder. Maybe the world *was* trying to give me a hint.

I wandered for a solid ten minutes before I stumbled upon a coffee shop. I ordered what I hoped passed for regular coffee and dumped in an unhealthy amount of sugar. I chose to sit by the window so I could admire the scene beyond while I immersed myself in the past. The caffeine jolt to my senses was enough to beat back the last of the jet lag as I turned to the pages right before the entry on Aoife. I wasn't sure what I hoped to find until I happened upon an entry detailing the rivalry between the two druid sects.

For many decades the blood of the land's wielders of power has spilled and stained these fields all for the right to use their gifts as they see fit. Some, as Aoife and her ilk argue, believe it must be used in the furtherance of humanity's prosperity and the betterment of the lowest among us. The opposing view, naturally, believes that those who possess the greatest power be permitted to use it to their own ends, for enrichment of their coffers and their bellies. To use it to rule those less inclined as servants. In this time, the darker sects underwent a brutal change of leaders as Bearach, the second in command, slew his teacher, Ciarán.

There was to be a convocation of the two leaders, where peace was sought. Except at the height of the fullest moon, it was Bearach and not Ciarán who sought to meet with Aoife, bringing with him a great power as if he were master of death. A great clash of wills nearly took the white witch's power, yet her own sect's gifts rose up to meet her in her time of need. From that day, never would the two sides seek to exist in peace. Such a time may never again come to pass.

"Well, damn," I muttered to myself, nearly spilling the half-empty cup of coffee on the very old text. The fight that the Authority had been having with the Order for centuries wasn't a new fight. It was one as old as cave men banging each other over the head with rocks to assert dominance. Despite that Aoife had been able to call upon her druid sect's power to stop this Bearach asshole from killing her.

"You aren't surprised by that are you?" Grandma's tone of disdain hit me hard and I nearly jumped out of the chair.

"Give a girl some warning next time," I grumbled through barely parted lips. "And no, I'm not. It does make me want to figure out what else there is to know about Aoife."

"Excuse me," a low female voice said from beside me.

I turned slowly, double checking to make sure I still had the Bluetooth in my ear. "Huh?"

"Sorry, don't mean to be rude or eavesdrop ... but you're mispronouncing that name."

"What name?"

She pointed to the book. "It's pronounced EE-fa."

I cleared my throat. "Thanks."

I downed the rest of the coffee in my cup and packed up the book. Maybe being out in public wasn't the best plan after all. I caught Grandma miming taking a hit from a cigarette as she tapped her chest and then pointing at the woman who'd interrupted our supernatural conversation. I rolled my eyes, but didn't argue. I was in a strange city with no real connections or protections if I got into trouble. I centered myself, letting the battle of wills from Iain's office become a distant memory. I studied the woman as I took longer than necessary to situate my bag.

No magical signature of any kind.

I stalked out of the shop before I uttered, "Happy now?"

"You can't be mad at me for watching out for you. She could have been some dark coven operative."

"Right, because correcting my pronunciation is going to lead to horrible pain and misery."

"Many ages ago, knowing a thing's true name held great power. Far more than it does now," Theodora added.

I was really starting to dislike being tag-teamed by the pair of them. If I needed an angel and a devil on my shoulder, I'd prefer Desmond and J.T. The instant they popped into my head a wave of guilt hit me. They'd come along to help, and I'd abandoned them to go off on my own. I thought I had a handle on being the lone wolf. Clearly, I still had work to do on learning to accept help.

"I'm going back to the hotel. Both of you can go away and give me some space."

Theodora vanished instantly. Grandma fell into step beside me. "I'm not that easy to get rid of."

"I came here with them for a reason," I said.

"To keep them safe. Which you seem to be accomplishing just fine so long as they stay where you put them."

"They're people, not dogs, Grandma," I snapped.

"Point still stands," she muttered.

"I appreciate what you did, snapping me out of my freak out. But I am strong and part of that strength means I have to figure this out. There's more to the puzzle and the picture's starting to become clear. But I have other allies to rely on. Ones with access to the internet and resources you don't have."

"Well, fine then," she huffed and disappeared, leaving me alone to find my way back to the hotel.

At least I could enjoy the afternoon breeze as I followed my phone's GPS all the way back to the tiny building. I stepped into the lobby and the hairs on the back of my neck stood straight up in warning. Forcing myself to take even breaths, I turned to the small sitting area by an out-of-use fireplace to find Iain Nobles lounging in one of the chairs.

"I told you I was good at finding people," he said with a smile. "We need to talk."

NINETEEN

The fact that he'd found our hotel this fast worried me. Either he'd followed us, or he had the ability to trace someone's magic in a similar fashion to me. If he'd come so soon, maybe he'd found the information we needed and wanted to share it out of a sense of urgency. I refused to accept that he was here to tell me he'd found zilch.

"As lovely as this lobby is, I'd be more inclined to have our discussion somewhere a bit more private." He stood and pointed to the stairs.

"Yeah, come on."

I led him up two flights of stairs and through the narrow hallway to the room we'd rented. I slid the key card into the lock and held my breath as I entered. I found J.T. lounging on the bed staring at his phone while Desmond sat at the desk, Avery's face filling his laptop screen.

"Glad you boys aren't naked," I announced and walked in, my older, Irish shadow stayed in the doorway, his foot blocking the door from shutting completely.

"And you've brought company," J.T. sat up and set his phone aside.

"And he's cute," Avery added with a wink clearly meant for Desmond.

A tickle from the spice of his magic hit my nose. He'd reapplied his glamour. Great, just what I needed.

"Why don't I let you get yourselves sorted? I'll wait in the hall," Iain offered, removing his foot and easing the door shut.

"Was your walk productive?" J.T. scooted off the bed to wrap an arm around my shoulders.

"Sort of." I turned my attention to Avery. "How is everything there? Please tell me something good."

"People are trying to stay inside, but we just got word that another family got hit. The Masons."

Damn it. That only leaves eight more families.

"I had Avery check and it seems like the Order may have some misinformation," Desmond said.

"What do you mean?"

"Well, according to the Authority's records, the Mason family joined the Council before the Montes family and from what I could gather from some old meeting minutes, the Mason's bloodline is much older."

"So, if the Order was trying to wipe out the younger bloodlines, they would have gone after Belladonna's family next," I filled in the gap.

"Now, we haven't been able to get in touch with Belladonna since you left. We aren't sure if she's just left town, figuring it was safer to not tell anyone her whereabouts," Avery began.

"Or maybe she's already been attacked, and we just don't know about it," I finished.

"But you're staying safe," Desmond said, giving his wife an earnest look.

"Yes. I'm hunkered down with my parents. Plus, we're not actually on the Council, so we're safe for now. Besides, you're off touring the world in search of meaning or whatever so they can't come after you either."

Even on another continent, this still felt like a personal violation that the Order continued to hurt people under my protection. I sensed the energy building up around me, crackling with the tart scent of burning sugar as my magic reacted to the negative emotions. I didn't stop the anger from washing over me and as a result, the lamp on the bedside table skidded half a foot toward the floor. J.T. caught it before it could smash to the ground—saving us an awkward explanation and whatever extra money we had on us—and set it down carefully.

"Sorry," I said, turning back to Avery. "You need to check in with Jacquie or Agent Cartwright.

They're supposed to be providing security to everyone. Have them email me what they know so I'm in the loop."

Avery's head bobbed out of frame. "Sure. You guys are planning on coming back soon, right?"

"As soon as we can," I replied, glancing over my shoulder at the closed door. Sooner if Iain had in fact found something that could help us.

"We should hear what the professor has to say. I'll call you when I can," Des said, bidding Avery goodbye.

The screen turned black as the call ended and I pulled the door open. Iain stood across the hall, leaning against the wall. "You can come in now."

"Bit cramped quarters, isn't it?" He commented, taking in our accommodations.

"It's what we could find on short notice," J.T. answered, irritation coloring his tone.

"You need to drop the glamour. I can't deal with all this macho bullshit right now," I said.

Iain coughed, but I felt the pressure of his spell disappear, leaving him far less handsome than he'd been mere moments ago. J.T.'s shoulders relaxed. Iain reached out a hand to J.T. "Right, we've not been introduced. Professor Iain Nobles, practitioner."

J.T. gave him a loose handshake. "J.T. Somers. Paramedic."

"You're a smart one, bringing the lads with useful

training along as your back-up," he said, giving me a smile.

"You said we needed to talk?" I prompted.

"I did. And we do." He glanced around the room. "Are you certain it's safe to speak openly here?"

Before I could act, spearmint washed over the room as Desmond set wards to keep prying ears away from our conversation. I was grateful someone else was bearing the magical load for the moment. It meant I could give Iain my full attention.

"I am now."

"Right, well, have you been able to learn anything about that ancestor of yours from the text I lent you?"

"Only that if this is her, she was nearly murdered by some guy named Bearach the Usurper and she had to take her druid sect's power to stop him."

"He sounds like a Barbarian," J.T. snickered.

"Not far off. His predecessor may have been a despicable man, but he at least had some code of honor according to the journals I've read. Bearach was just a brute who wanted his own way and was happy to murder even his own kin to get it," Iain explained.

"You seem to know quite a bit about the history of these sects. More than I would expect from a university professor who isn't teaching history," I noted.

"One need not be a professor of history to be a proper student of it. Like your current quest, I am intrigued by the origins of magic in this place. It's rich and deep, down to the roots of what makes this country what it is."

"He's not wrong, though. This Bearach guy seemed to casually slaughter even his own buddies to gain power. Makes me wonder if he was one of the druids the Order was trying to bring back," I said. For a moment I mused on what would have happened if they'd succeeded. Would Bearach have complied with whatever the Order demanded of him? Would they have bowed to his power? Or would he have gone on a murderous rampage to eliminate the competition within the ranks before turning his attention to the rest of us.

"Could have been. But I suppose we should all take solace in the fact that the Order was unsuccessful, just as Bearach was so many centuries ago in snuffing out Aoife's life," Iain commented. "After all, had she perished, I suspect we would not be standing here having this discussion."

"She was seeking peace with this other guy, Ciarán, before he got killed. The book said there was never another chance at peace after that. Why not? Didn't anyone ever try?"

"I can't say for certain, having not been alive and all that, but I'd wager given Bearach's vicious ways, I doubt anyone was really keen to co-exist with him," Iain answered.

"I'm guessing the Order and the Authority remained at odds, because both groups have their origins here and in England," J.T. interjected.

I arched a brow at him, and he smiled. "I can know things, too."

"I can't imagine that making peace with the Order is going to save the day. They wouldn't listen to reason," I replied.

"What is it this Order seeks?" Iain perched on the end of the bed closest to the door.

"Kill, maim, abuse people? I don't know." I threw up my hands. "I guess I never thought much about it."

"Therein may lie part of your problem. If you don't know their goals and aims, it's quite hard to stop them. And to know that they are truly not aligned with your own."

"They strong-armed a man into committing murder for them so they could resurrect those ancient Druids. I don't see how that could ever be aligned with wanting to protect people," I said, dismissing his statement.

"Didn't you say that Lola just wanted to use her magic as she saw fit?" Desmond offered from across the room.

"I mean, we'd all like to use magic for whatever we want. Nevertheless, the rules are there to keep people from going too far, from hurting other people."

"Noble goals, certainly, but who is to say that your rules are the right ones or the best?" Iain challenged. "If you've not determined what it is they want, how can you say with absolute certainty that you are right and they are wrong?"

"You can't possibly be defending murderers," I snapped.

"I can't defend their actions, but what motivates them, that I cannot say I approve or not. Because, as you say, you don't know."

I shook my head and began to pace the length of the room. The tension was palpable, making the air thick and hard to breathe. The room suddenly seemed the size of a clown car filled with one too many clowns.

"Ez, take a breath," J.T. said, catching my hand in his. His magic slipped between our fingers like real honey, sticking him to me and easing the anxiety taking root in my mind.

"I apologize for upsetting you, but if you're to understand what you face, what you are trying to protect your people from, you might want to dig deeper into what your enemies desire and how they plan to achieve it."

"That's what I'm trying to do," I grumbled, turning my back on Iain.

"Why don't we put aside figuring out what the

Order wants for a minute and see what we can figure out about how to solve the more immediate problem of them stealing magic?" Desmond suggested.

"Aye, I might have a bit of information that could help you there. It's why I came here," Iain said.

I didn't want to turn back and give him my attention. My pride was wounded, and I felt like he'd been scolding me for being a stupid child. Even so if he had useful information I could act on *now*, I'd take it.

"What did you find?"

"So, going off the theory that the Aoife in my texts is your ancestor, and the reference you had to what sounds like a group ritual, it led me to Uisneach."

Desmond, J.T., and I stared at him in silence. He had this proud expression on his face, and we had literally no damn idea what he was talking about. I couldn't even be sure all the words he'd just said were actual words.

"Right, Americans. Uisneach is an ancient ritual space that holds a lot of power not just for our practitioners, but those who are in tune with nature. It's thought to be the geographic center of the country and it was where the druid sects would come together to do their mass rituals."

"Would that ill-fated meeting between Aoife and Bearach have taken place there?" I relinquished my grip on J.T.'s hand.

"That I cannot say. If anything, I'd expect they would have wished to meet on neutral territory and Uisneach is anything but neutral. I suppose it could boost either or both of their powers given the right conditions."

"Like the full moon or one of the changes in the seasons," I said mostly to myself. I retrieved the book from my bag and handed it over. "Can you take us there?"

"Look, if you're hoping to commune with the long dead, you aren't going to want to be there during the day and I've got lectures in the morning. It's well over an hour and thirty minutes without traffic."

"We don't have time to get lost on our own. Please. People's lives, whole families, are in danger."

"All right. Fine. Give me an hour."

It wasn't time we had to waste, but if it meant having Iain take us, I'd deal with it.

TWENTY

The wait for Iain to come back seemed an eternity. I went from pacing our little room, to staring aimlessly out the window.

"We're going to figure it out," J.T. said, stroking my hair.

"Besides, if anyone can shoulder this, it's you. You are the Savior after all," Desmond added, that tinge of jealousy creeping back in.

"Your inferiority complex is showing," I teased. After a moment I added, "As much as I like the ego boost guys, I'm worried. And scared that this won't be enough. Or it will be too little too late." Beside me, my phone buzzed with an incoming text message. I cringed at the thought of international messaging rates.

It was a short message from Molly. 'No luck

locating Ms. Montes. So far, no new attacks since last update."

"They still can't find Belladonna," I shared. "If the FBI and police can't track her down, she must really be hiding."

"Man, to lose her son and then possibly her magic. I can't imagine the sort of pain that could inflict," J.T. murmured.

Death, a female voice whispered in the back of my head. A voice I didn't recognize.

I rubbed at the base of my skull, as if doing so would make the voice shut up or become clearer. It did neither of those things. "What if she reached out to her ex-husband?"

"You think they'd really be on speaking terms after what happened to Adrian?" Desmond arched a brow.

"What if, his family's magic could somehow make it appear like her bloodline was already dead? I don't know, like mask her magical signature or something?"

"I think the rest of her family either moved away or died a while ago, so it could just be her now," Desmond murmured, rubbing at his chin. "I don't know if magic could work like that, but anything's possible."

There was something else gnawing at the back of my mind ... something else about death that was supposed to be important, but for the life of me I couldn't connect the dots. I was about to admit the fact I knew I was missing something when a knock interrupted the conversation. J.T. vaulted over the bed and pulled it open. Iain stood on the other side in a windbreaker and a flashlight in his hand.

"If we're going to do this, I suppose we better get on the road."

We followed him out of the hotel, down the street and through an unmarked alley to a silver four-door sedan. Desmond and J.T. climbed in back, leaving me no choice, but to sit up front with Iain. I settled in the passenger seat and we'd soon left the streets of Dublin behind.

It wasn't long before we were out of decent cellphone range, open road ahead of and behind us. I tried to remind myself to enjoy the beauty of this place, but my mind kept churning things over and over. How every member of the Council lost was one less ally I could call upon. Even though my bloodline might trace back to this insanely powerful sect leader, I still didn't know how it would help me save the people who depended on me or defeat whatever bat shit crazy plan the Order had cooking.

"If you don't mind me asking, you mentioned a prophecy is in play here," Iain's voice broke the silence in the car.

"Yeah. Seems to be a pattern with me. Finish one, another pops up to take its place."

"In all of my research, I've never come across prophecy following one person."

"Well, how many magical saviors have you come across?" I scoffed.

"I'm assuming you understand the rarity of such visions?"

There he goes, treating me like a stupid child again. "Yes, and I'm also aware that it's even rarer to happen in people like us."

He glanced at me for a moment. "Like us?"

I gestured around the car. "White people. I learned recently that the Afro-Hispanic portion of the community tends to be gifted with foresight and premonition."

"Oh, I see. May I ask how you came to learn that?"

"The Order, you're so fond of trying to human-ize, kidnapped three young girls hoping one of them would see the future they were after. They found what they wanted, but not before torturing three kids for good measure." I hooked a thumb over my shoulder in Desmond's direction. "He's been trying to heal their minds for months."

"I didn't mean to make you think I like these Order blokes or believe in their methods. But you have to wonder if we believe that rules ought to be followed because history is written by the victors." He went quiet for a moment. "Clearly, Aoife and her coven won whatever battle they waged against

Bearach and his ilk. They drove them from this place, and it sounds like right to your shores in America."

"Thanks for that," I grumbled.

"All I'm saying is, being able to freely and openly practice one's craft is an enticing proposition."

It had wooed Agent Taggart to the dark side. He'd been one of us back when he was growing up. Despite that he'd chafed against the strictness and secrecy that the Authority placed on us. I'd be lying if I hadn't considered wanting to use magic more openly. As it was, I flaunted the rules on a fairly regular basis, bringing my law enforcement contacts in on the truth without permission. Somehow that had escaped the Council's notice. Or they just didn't want to piss me off.

"I guess you're right."

"So, how long did it take you to solve this first prophecy?"

"Like four hundred years," I said with a bitter laugh.

"I reckon we haven't got four centuries to sort out this new one, eh?"

"Maybe three months." I leaned my head against the window, watching the sky begin to darken and take on alluring shades of purple and navy. It was so unlike the skies in Boston. Yet that sense of famil-iarity and home washed over me again. I rolled down the window and let the fresh air fill my lungs.

"Well, what's it say then?"

"Hmm?"

"This prophecy. We've got at least an hour. Might as well be useful and try to suss out what we can."

The answer came out of my mouth on autopilot. "When Darkness reaches its height, and Death's child reigns, the last of Harrow's blood must flow forever more or the life blood of the world will be no more."

"Bit wordy, isn't it? And why so cryptic?" Iain said with a broad grin.

Truer words had never been spoken. I wasn't sure Des or J.T. had been listening to the conversation, but both of them burst out laughing. Their response was infectious, because in a matter of seconds, I was bracing myself against the car door laughing, too.

"Prophecy never says things in just plain English," I said as I gasped for air.

"I mean, sure I can understand Eleanor's prophecy being all cryptic like it was because she came from the seventeenth century ... but Neveah's?" Desmond interjected.

"I think the universe doesn't want to make it too easy," J.T. said, sobering from his laughter.

"How so?" Iain eased up on the gas as we approached a sharp curve in the road.

"If it was too easy, there'd be no drive to solve it

and stop it from happening if you're on the receiving end and I don't know ... maybe the universe wants there to be that balance between light and dark magic. One can't really exist without the other. So, these prophecies are hard to decipher and take people working together to figure it out."

"Your lad's got a good point." Iain leaned over. "And a good head on his shoulders to boot."

"We've been through a lot," I whispered back.

"The great loves have," he said, taking the turn slow and steady.

I exhaled once we were back on straight road, unaware I'd been holding in a breath. "So, yeah, that's what we're dealing with. Based on Eleanor's prophecy from before, we know a few pieces of the puzzle. Harrow's blood means me. I'm the last living descendant of Theodora Harrow. And darkness being at its height has to mean the Winter Solstice in December."

"So you may have a bleak winter upon you."

"It's not looking great. But I don't know what this death's child thing means or what my blood has to do with the life blood of the world or how that's going to stop whatever is coming.'

A shadow passed over Iain's expression, but I couldn't tell what it meant. I didn't know him well enough to decode it or the fact he went silent. I didn't get happy vibes from his suddenly stoic behavior. Although it could be he was puzzling over what

I'd said and needed some quiet to figure it out. Finally, after what felt like forever, the silence grated on my nerves.

"You have something to say. I can see it on your face. Just say it."

The car slowed down despite the fact I couldn't see any other curves or cars that would signal a need to kill our forward momentum. "I have an idea of what it might be asking of you, but you're not going to like it. And this is just from the research I've done through the sect's journals and records."

"Which is a long-winded way of saying what exactly?" I prodded.

"That you may need to make a personal sacrifice ... the kind that involves blood to stop what is coming."

"Because of course it does,' I muttered. Now understanding why he had slowed down, in case I lost my shit.

"But you can survive that," J.T. piped up, reaching awkwardly over the seat to pat my shoulder.

I clung to his belief that I'd be fine. I needed something positive ahead of me to keep me from spiraling. Yet I still felt this cloud of darkness hovering over this entire trip. "Any thoughts on what this whole death's child thing is about?"

"That, I'm afraid not. It's not a term I've come across before." He nodded behind us. "I brought a bit of light reading while you three go exploring. I'll see if there's anything I can find."

As the drive continued, I longed to be prodded by Grandma, even if she was being judgmental. Just something to distract me from the idea that the universe was going to ask far more of me than it ever had. *Why do you want my blood now?*

I drifted into a light doze as the car trundled onward, lulling me into an uneasy rest. When I opened my eyes, I found myself no longer in the car. I stood in a field by a large stone. The distant sound of voices cascaded over my senses, but I couldn't make out the words. I looked for the woman I'd seen in the other visions, but she wasn't there either.

"Whatever this is, I'm done playing games. Give up the hide and seek bullshit," I called to empty air around me.

"You always were an impatient child," Grandma said.

"What are you doing here?"

She shrugged and took off her aviators, looping them through the top button of her blouse and settled on the rock. She patted the hard surface in the universal gesture for 'sit your ass on this damn rock and listen up.' I sat.

"I know you were expecting some ancient wonderful druid leader to show up and give you all the answers, Ezzie, but you're not there yet. You need to have a little patience."

"People are in danger and I'm supposed to help them. I can't do that if I don't know how to fight what they're doing."

"Sometimes we can't fight everything bad in the world. Remember that. You're putting so much pressure on yourself to be the one who makes it better for everyone else." She held up a hand to keep me from saying anything. "I get it, Savior and all. But you cannot be all things to all people all the damn time. It's okay to just be Ezri."

She looked at me and toyed with the hem of her blouse. "You got anything to say to that?"

"I wasn't sure you were done," I leaned back on the rock. "You say I should just be me, but I am the Savior. I've never been just Ezri. I've been Ezri the cop and Ezri the witch, but those have always been about protecting other people. If I don't figure out how to stop the Order, I'll be letting not just J.T., Desmond, and the Council down, but the rest of the magical community."

"You know, I'm glad I was dead before you really learned the truth. Your mother put too much pressure on you as a kid. And for the record, you wouldn't be letting everyone down. You'd be trying your best."

"What if my best isn't good enough? What if I don't stop what's coming?"

"Maybe that's for someone else to figure out? Maybe you're just one piece of the puzzle in all of this. Yes, you've got more power than most and you are trying to do good with it. But this has never been a solo sport, sweetheart. Sometimes you forget that."

I'd let people in. I'd forgiven Desmond for keeping the secret about my mother's sacrifice and siding with the magical community. I'd even repaired my relationship with my dad. I'd brought back-up with me this time. When I knew six months ago, I would have raced off alone, not telling anyone where I was going or what I was doing. I wasn't alone. Yet, it still felt like there was very little they could do to help. Sure, they could both help heal any wounds—mental or physical—that came my way, but I wasn't going to risk them getting in the line of fire.

"I know you're trying to work through it all in that head of yours. But can you make an old dead lady a promise?" Grandma wrapped her fingers over mine and squeezed tight.

"Promises aren't exactly the best idea in my line of work."

"Well then, try to keep an open mind with whatever happens here. It may not be what you want to hear, and it may not give you the answers you think you need. Even though it's going to be what you need to hear."

"I'll try."

"Good. We both know your mom would have said it, but she's not around, so I had to carry that particular burden."

"You know, I didn't realize how much I missed you until you showed up." I leaned my head on her shoulder, fighting back tears.

"I know, sweetie. I know." She wrapped her arms around me and held on tight. For the briefest of moments it was like I was five years old again, sitting in her lap while she told silly stories of magic. "Now, be a good girl and wake up."

TWENTY-ONE

I jolted awake to find the car had stopped moving. The sky outside had dwindled to a dark blue and the headlights illuminated a large open area ahead of us. There weren't any fences keeping people away, but I could sense that we weren't really supposed to be here right now.

"So, where are we supposed to go?" Desmond asked.

I tried to shake the disorientation from my system as Iain's magic wafted over me. My own magic bristled at the unfamiliarity of his presence.

"Hate to be a bother, but could you calm down? I'm trying to make sure no one sees us." Iain's brow furrowed in concentration.

"Sorry. It's habit. I'm not used to your magic and I think I'm still a little jumpy from what happened at your office."

"New surroundings and all, I understand. Just, I'm not used to encountering someone's magic trying to stop me."

Instead of tamping down on my power, I let a little more flow from me and wash over the exterior of the car, boosting his intent to keep us hidden. "How about a little signal boost?"

"Won't argue with that."

"Now, Desmond has a point. Where are we supposed to be going?" I directed the question to Iain.

"You're the one having visions of long-dead druids. I assumed you'd know once we arrived," he answered.

I turned in the passenger seat and fixed Iain with an incredulous look. "Seriously? You're supposed to be the historical expert. You told us this was the place we needed to go."

"Based on the vague information you passed along." Iain's voice rose.

"Before tempers get out of control, why don't we get out and just take a look around," Desmond intervened. "I don't think any of us can argue that the magic in Ireland is stronger, or older. Whatever it is, we can all feel it. If this is the right place, I have a feeling Ezri is going to know."

"Fine." I undid the seatbelt and climbed out into the autumn night air.

I expected to be bowled over by magic everywhere, if this was indeed the site he claimed was the place that Aoife and Bearach faced off. However, it didn't feel any different from Dublin. Less crowded and less urban maybe, but nothing special.

Iain leaned over to the passenger side and called through the still-open window, "I'll stay with the car once you lads vacate."

Desmond and J.T. were soon by my side. The car vanished with just an extra hint of Iain's magic and I couldn't help but let out an amused sound. J.T. looped his hand through mine.

"Let's take a look around."

We wandered three-by-three and the farther we went from where Iain sat in the car, the easier it was to pick up on the magic running through this place. Everything in the world carried some bits of magic in it, but with every step it was as if it grew stronger, begging for my attention. *Seek me out*, it called to me just like the woman in the vision. Maybe we were on the right path.

"Is that a rock?" Desmond pointed ahead of us.

I squinted in the darkness and without even voicing my need, my vision sharpened. The large stone came into view and I could swear a seated figure waited.

"We're in the right place," I announced just as I felt J.T.'s hand rip from my own.

I turned to see why he'd let go when I realized that he and Desmond were gone. The sky above me and the air around me grew heavy with saturation like right before a heavy rainfall. Except there were no storm clouds above me. It was still night, but earlier in the evening. Or maybe the skyline had less pollution from humanity growing up around it.

I raised a hand and pushed against the air in front of me. I'd seen magic like this before when the Order had tried to resurrect the other druid sect. An unseen barrier, I'd felt it then and been able to tear a hole into it, bring it down around us like unraveling a sweater. My fingers pressed against something solid and I could just make out J.T. and Desmond lying unconscious on their backs in the grass.

"Forgive me, but this is meant for one and one alone," a low alto voice said.

"What did you do to them?" I demanded, strawberry rippling off my skin, fortifying me.

"They have not come to harm. They are merely sleeping. They will not realize time has passed. It is safer that way."

"Safer for whom?" I took a few steps closer to the woman seated on the stone. She still wouldn't' face me.

"All in the end." She turned slowly and I gasped at the similarity in her bone structure and coloring. It was like looking in a mirror or one of those aging programs that predicted what someone would look like in twenty years.

"You're Aoife, aren't you?"

She beckoned me forward, the pentacle pendant hanging around her neck, still devoid of the center stone.

"And you are the heir of my blood and my gifts. Come sit." She had to be speaking a language I didn't know, but my brain heard her words as English.

I chanced one more glance back at the hazy vision of Desmond and J.T. before closing the distance to sit on the grass in front of her. I kept a good foot of space between us still. Someone who would sideline my only allies made my hackles rise, even if she was supposed to be my ancestor.

Her gaze softened as she took in my straight-backed posture. "You question whether you are being deceived."

"So, you're a mind reader now, too?"

"I have called to you across many centuries, child. I have a great many gifts that you cannot fathom. And I know what distrust does to a body."

"We have a genealogy of our family tree. You have a death date. How are you here right now?"

She tapped her pentacle necklace and before I knew what was happening, I pressed a finger to mine as well. "By now you have determined that this vessel contains great power."

"Every one of my ancestors from the Witch Trials through to my mother contributed some of their magic to it. I don't understand the mechanics, but it allows a piece of them to stay with me until I use up the magic."

"Indeed. As you have correctly surmised, I am quite powerful. In part because of the gift my sect mates gave to me on the eve of what would have been my death."

"They gave you their power to stop Bearach," I said.

"Yes. I fear I was fated to die that day, but I acted to prevent it and now, so many years later, you have come to pay the price."

"I don't understand."

She held out her hands, as if she were cupping two objects. "Balance is always to be maintained in this world or in any other. For good to be done, there must be a counter to it. We may not wish it to be so, but we cannot exist without our mirror."

"But, if I was supposed to stop the darkness from rising, what's the point if it's supposed to be there anyway? None of this makes any sense."

"For you see, while a balance must always exist, my actions put too much good into the world."

"That's not a thing. That can't be a thing. You went on to help people. You protected them just like I do."

"I fear that is not so." She hung her head, dark red strands cascading over her pale features. "You see, I have long believed that my death was meant to serve a purpose. Perhaps it would have led those who followed Bearach to revolt against his stranglehold upon them. There could have been a sort of peace forged. But I let my own fears of the unknown persuade me to take the magic of those with whom I practiced. It afforded me immense strength enough to survive Bearach's blade." She toyed with the pendant at her throat. "My mistake may have cost a great many undue pain and hardship."

Before I could respond, the world around us changed. The sky brightened and darkened in rapid succession, like we were watching a time-lapse of a day in reverse.

It sped past, people and images flashed by until I spotted Aoife standing in the distance surrounded by a group of men and women, many of them about my age. The men wore tunics and loose-fitting pants while the women were dressed in flowing gowns and corsets. Logically I knew I wasn't part of this memory and yet I could feel the tension brewing among the group assembled.

"Aoife, we cannot trust them," a man with a thick beard that fell to his chest argued.

"If we do not try to broker peace with them, then our efforts to protect the peoples of this land are for naught. His followers deserve a chance to see the light, to use their gifts for the betterment of all," Aoife replied in a calm, measured tone.

A young girl, no more than twelve or thirteen, with flowing blond hair raced across the grass her eyes wide with fear. She skidded to a halt and bent double to catch her breath. "There has been a great battle. Ciarán has been slain."

"By whose magic?" Aoife demanded, lifting the girl's chin so their eyes met.

"Not by craft. By blade." Her chest rose and fell in quick succession as she still struggled to breathe. The dark brown of her dress brought out the dark brown flecks in her hazel eyes. "His second-in-command, Bearach. I have seen it this hour. He has cut Ciarán's throat and usurped the leadership of their sect."

The bearded man stepped up to Aoife. "Your dream of peace is dead along with him."

Aoife shook her head. "We will not know for certain until they arrive." Despite the resolve in her tone, I could see the slight quiver of her lower lip and the hitch in her step as she moved past the messenger girl to meet the oncoming adversaries.

I turned to follow her, and the scene sped up again. Bearach and his followers had arrived, spread around him like chess pieces protecting the king and queen. Aoife stood apart from her people.

"There will be no peace this day," Bearach boomed in a deep bass voice. It sent shivers down my spine. I wrapped my arms around my torso to ward off the chill.

I'd never had any real proof that the druid the Order had been trying to raise was Bearach, but I could sense somehow even in this memory that it was him I'd beaten back into the ether. The look of pure disdain in his dark grey pupils was the same I'd seen in the woman who'd offered herself as his vessel. It had been cruel then and it was even icier now. He held a blade in his hand. I could see the blood stains still dripping from it in a bright red gloss. I also spotted something hanging around his neck. Swallowing back the fear that he'd somehow mounted a dead man's head on a necklace, I peered close enough to see it was some sort of crystal.

"Reconsider your actions, Bearach," Aoife said softly.

Bearach threw back his head and laughed. Some of his followers joined suit, but it died out quickly. The bearded man stepped up to Aoife's side. "Let us end this madness. The longer we remain, the more danger we bring to those we owe our protection."

"Listen to your second," Bearach said with a dismissive wave. "Or perhaps he should like the taste of leadership?"

Bearach lunged and his blade sliced across Aoife's chest. I winced, reflexively touching the spot on my own chest. She staggered back, gaping in silent horror at the wound. I could see wisps of grey shimmer in the air, dancing toward Bearach and the amulet around his neck. Aoife's legs gave out and she fell back into the arms of the bearded man.

"No, my love. I cannot lose you."

She looked up at him. "Give me strength, dear husband. My sweet Padraig."

Another woman rushed to her side, brushing strands of hair away.

"Dear cousin," Aoife murmured. "My sweet Emerys, forgive me for I have been foolish."

"Save your strength and your breath," Emerys replied.

Padraig turned to the other members of the sect. "We must not let her perish by that tyrant's blade!"

All at once they surrounded her and a visible barrier sprang up between the two groups. Padraig cradled Aoife's head in his lap as Emerys stepped away and joined the others as they formed a chain, each holding hands. Blinding white light flowed from each of them into Aoife's prone body. A cacophony of scents assaulted my nose and my head spun as my brain fought to sort them out, to follow each branch of magic. The wound in Aoife's chest sealed up as if it had never been there and she rose into the air, arms outstretched from her sides. A massive wave of oak scented energy slammed into her enemy, sending Bearach flying halfway across the field. Aoife's feet hovered a few inches off the ground as she advanced on him. The power rippling off her skin like a heat haze bowled me over, making my head and body ache just trying to take it all in.

"You were correct of one thing, this day. There will be no peace. Go now. I spare you. We will be *watching." The change in her power level deepened her already low voice.*

The scene disappeared and we were back in the field in the darkness of night. I sat for a moment in silence as the images receded and flashes of blinding light no longer seared my eyelids when I closed my eyes. I clawed for the sandalwood charm at my throat, in desperate need to beat back too many magical signatures. My hands shook as I found the smooth surface and let it's cleansing power wash away all I had witnessed.

When I could think and see straight again, I said, "You feel guilty about surviving and letting him live? He wanted to murder you and you defended yourself. That's not cowardice. That's self-preservation."

"In your view, I can see how it would seem to be so. But my continued life meant that Bearach lived unchecked and unchallenged for decades. He carried death with him that day and it has grown stronger all these years. He may have stopped walking this earth many centuries ago, but that power he amassed remains."

"Death's child. Is that what this new prophecy is talking about? Whatever magic he used to take out his predecessor and you turned ... sentient?"

"In a way, I suppose it is. It is contained within the amulet he wore."

Great, more mystical jewelry in play. A part of me felt a little slighted that the Order had a magical object like my pentacle in its possession. I knew it was foolish and juvenile to feel like they were copying me, but the feeling still surfaced for a brief moment. "So, it's coming in three months to try and kick my ass and what ... I have to shed some blood to put a stop to it once and for all? Will that tip the scales or whatever back to where they should be? To fix your mistake?"

Her olive-green eyes shown with unshed tears and she reached out for my hands. "I never expected such a powerful practitioner would come of my bloodline. Or that my own actions would require such a burden be placed on you. I am gravely sorry I could not have spared you the fate that awaits you."

"You used the power of other people to stop Bearach. I can do that, too. It would leave me without any back-up power, but I have to believe they gave a little of their power for that purpose."

"You were created to channel great power, indeed. An entire bloodline as it happens."

"One small problem there. I could feel bits and pieces of other people when I touched the genealogy. Whatever magic you used on it gave me a hint that I needed to seek you out. But you aren't in the pendant."

"Do you wonder why mine bears no stone?"

I nodded. "I saw you creating it in one of the visions. I just assumed it was what allowed the other people to pour their magic in."

"Very good." She undid the clasp at the nape of her neck and slid the second necklace over mine. "I have spent centuries imbuing this with my own power in preparation for this meeting." A look of sadness fell over her like a shadow. "I often fear it will not be enough to aid you in what is to come."

For a split second the two pentacles repelled each other like magnets with the same poles trying to push against each other. Aoife leaned over and pressed her palm to my chest. The oaky scent of her magic permeated my nose and coated the back of my throat. When she pulled her hand away, there was only one pentacle. The diamond in the center was tinged by a faint bit of pink.

"You now carry my gift within you, child of my blood. It is within you to set the balance right again and heal what I could not."

"While you're dispensing advice, you want to tell me what exactly this confrontation is going to look like?"

She gave a sad smile. "I am afraid unlike your dear Eleanor, I do not possess the gift of foresight. It would seem the world knew it needed to warn of what was to come so a suitable heir would be born to take up the mantle of Savior. Therefore, our bloodline deviated from what was common to ensure our bloodline survived and Eleanor received the gift of prophecy."

"So much for Grandma's theory that I should just try being plain old Ezri for a while."

"There will be time aplenty to be just you," Aoife's eyes grew misty again.

"I don't know how much you know about what else is going on in the world. Are we like psychically connected or something?"

Confusion washed over her. "My magic knew enough to seek out your own. But what transpires in your time is a mystery to me, much as mine is to you."

"The Order ... my version of Bearach's druid sect I guess, has been stealing magic from the families of the people in my sect. The people I'd rely on and call on to help me if I needed it. Whatever spell is being used, it's stripping the magic out of their bloodline and altering their memories, so they don't know what happened in the attacks."

"Stolen magic carries with it a heavy price. It can twist against the practitioner who takes it on as their own. Any person taking on such magic would likely no longer be human."

"Sounds wickedly terrifying. Look, I know they're collecting it for some purpose, and I have to believe it's to do with the coming fight."

"Removing a person's magic is a violation down to their very soul. It leaves a wound that can only be healed by the return of that magic. But only if it has not passed to another willing vessel."

"So, as long as it's still in the container they siphoned it into, there's a chance I can return it?"

"Yes."

"Great. How do I do that?"

"Did you not have a teacher to guide you in your practice? Would you not be better served to seek this from a contemporary?"

"My mother was my teacher. She died when I was a teenager. She sacrificed herself to give me more protection from having to the save the world." I answered, bitterness making my words sharp. "Anyone else I'd go to is a target, has already been victimized or has gone missing. So, you're all I've got."

"I see." Aoife clasped her hands together and pressed them to her chest. "Even when magic is torn from a person, the capacity of it remains. The body and the mind remember what it feels like to use one's gift. The comfort it provides, the familiarity. It leaves behind a seed deep within. Provided you have the purloined magic and it has not been transferred to a willing vessel, you can call to that seed and foster it to grow again."

"Is there any way I can protect someone from having their magic taken? I know I'm running out of time and low on allies, but I have to try to do something."

"It is possible to bind their magic to an object."

I couldn't help but feel skeptical about her

suggestion. "Couldn't whoever is after it just take the object and achieve the same result?"

"Not if it is willingly bound." She arched a brow. "And one should never keep such an object on one's person. That only invites danger." Aoife laughed, throwing her head back as the sound travelled up into the night air, being swallowed by the darkness and whatever spell was fueling our meeting. "Securing it somewhere that is hidden from the knowledge of outsiders is the only way to protect it."

"Okay." I stood up and began to pace, fingering the pendant at my throat. "Let me see if I've got all of this straight." I ticked things off on my fingers. "I'm basically supposed to fight some weird death incarnate monster created hundreds of years ago. It might be too late to return the magic to some of the families and the others need to find some sort of object to bind their magic to before they become victims, too. Did I miss anything?"

"The protection will be stronger with your magic binding it as well," Aoife said and stood up to grab my hands in hers, stopping my momentum.

"Just another thing to worry about that I don't have enough time to complete," I sighed.

Relinquishing one hand, she cupped her cheek. "Even when the darkness encroaches and seems to last forever, there is always room for the light to spread and shine. You will be that light. Of that I have no doubt."

"I wish I felt the same way. Everything has felt so … hopeless right now, like nothing I do is going to be good enough."

"You must not lose hope or faith, child. You were made for a greater purpose. As the seer child's words say, your blood will flow forevermore and the life blood of the world's magic shall be saved. Have faith and remember, I am with you now and forever."

Aoife vanished, knocking the wind out of my lungs and sending me backward, slamming my head into the ground. The world blinked in and out of focus briefly before going completely black.

SEPTEMBER 20, 2017

A blast of a semi-familiar scent assaulted my nose, rousing me from what felt like a very shitty nap. I opened my eyes and winced at the bright light of Iain's flashlight on his phone.

"What the hell was that for?" I groaned and looked around.

Desmond and J.T. were still both laying on the ground and they began to stir. The night's events came crashing back to me and as I sat up, I winced at the headache it gave me. Iain put a hand on my shoulder and started to haul me to my feet.

"I can stand up on my own, thanks," I said and pulled free of his grasp.

"I'm sorry, but you've been out here for hours. It's past midnight. We need to leave or else we're going to risk getting arrested."

"But no one's out here and the car was hidden," I

said, rubbing the base of my skull which had begun to ache.

"I could only sustain it for so long."

"All that glamour really took it out of you?" I goaded.

"That's a minor spell by comparison and it's not meant to hide so much as enhance what's already present."

I didn't bother responding to him. Instead, I focused on getting Desmond and J.T. on their feet and moving toward the car. I wrapped my hands around J.T.'s bicep and pulled him upward. He blinked at me, dazed and looking so very cute.

"What happened?" He looked around and then down at his phone. "I'm reading this wrong, right? We haven't been out here for hours."

"I'll explain in the car. Come on. Getting our asses arrested for trespassing in a foreign country is not going to do us any favors."

Desmond rubbed at his head as he scrambled to his feet. Together, our group of four weaved our way back to the waiting car, which was indeed very visible. I crawled into the backseat this time. Desmond slid in front and J.T. settled beside me, pulling me over to lean on his shoulder. As Iain pulled a U-turn and headed back the way we'd travelled, I tried to figure out how to put into words what had happened and everything Aoife had shared with me.

"Can someone please explain how we lost like

five hours of time? The last thing I remember was walking toward that stone. Then ... nothing," J.T. said, forcing me to crane my neck painfully to look at him.

"I think it was part of Aoife's spell. I'm not sure exactly, but it was only meant for me to be able to enter. Maybe it really was five hours of time that I spent with her. Honestly, I couldn't tell you. It felt like an eternity and no time at all."

"You actually met Aoife? How is that possible?" Iain's voice filled the car, excitement beating back some of the weariness of the late hour.

"Yes and no. It's complicated. She somehow managed to freeze herself in time or something. I should have asked, but I was focused on what information she had to share about how to stop the Order, so I didn't ask." My right hand drifted to touch the stone at the heart of the pentacle. "It was her magic. That much I'm sure of and now ... it's within me."

"So, you're channeling an ancient and powerful druid of your own, now. Something tells me you're going to kick the Order's ass," J.T. said, stroking my hair.

"It doesn't come without a price." *Magic never does.* "If I use her power, that's it. It's gone and I can never get it back. It's the same rules that apply for the rest of the family. At least that's how she explained it to me."

"Did she give any usable information to help our

current problem?" Desmond's voice was soft, tired. His reflection in the rearview mirror showed pinched lines around his mouth and eyes. *What did he see while he was knocked out?*

"Yeah, she did," I answered through a yawn.

"We've got quite a drive back to the city, lass. Don't keep us in suspense the whole ride," Iain chided.

"Their magic is still out there. As long as we can get our hands on the containers before the magic is transferred, I can return it. She told me how to protect the rest of our magic, too. So, that they can't take it away again."

"When we get back to the hotel, I'm going to do a video call with Avery. Get her started on whatever needs to happen," Desmond said, sitting up straighter in the seat.

"It's going to be late by the time we get back. And I have to be there. It needs my magic to secure it. At least that's what she said." I checked my phone for any missed messages while I was spirited away to the past. I half-expected an update from Dad or at the very least a voicemail checking in. I needed to call Jacquie when we were back on Wi-Fi. The late hour started to pull at my brain, urging me to sleep.

"What was she like?" Iain's voice disrupted any thought of a road trip nap.

"Intense. Guilt-ridden. Apologetic," I mumbled, fighting to stay awake.

"More than single word answers would be helpful," J.T. prompted, nudging me with his shoulder.

"You two may have been knocked out, but I wasn't. Not the whole time, anyway. I'm tired. I need rest. I need to process things. I promise, when we get back to the hotel, I'll explain what I can."

I STOOD IN A LARGE FIELD, *with grass reaching as far as the eye could see. The tiny hairs on the nape of my neck stood on edge and I turned, bringing my hands up into balled fists to defend myself. Nothing was there, but the sense of danger danced along my skin, making each hair stand on end in succession.*

"You believe yourself a worthy adversary?" An eerie voice called from behind me.

Pivoting back to the direction I'd been facing, I spied a cloaked figure, its face obscured in shadow. Except the sun shone high above us. I took a reflexive step back from the figure, but the distance shrunk in response. I took another step back and my heel caught on something rough and hard. A glance down told me it was the same stone I'd seen Aoife sitting on, waiting for me. Where was she?

"What are you?" I called; my voice carried way on the wind.

"I am what you fear. I am what awaits you in the

end. Soon, I will rise victorious and those you hold most dear will feel my wrath."

This time I stepped forward. I was toe-to-toe with the figure and still shadows shrouded their face. "You aren't going to touch anyone I care about. You seem to be operating under the delusion that I'm going to stop fighting or give up."

The figure shook its head. "I know you, Savior. You believe your path is righteous and correct. You had a choice once, a divergent path you could have taken."

The world around me rippled and I watched as fifteen-year-old me railed against my mother's death. She pushed the people she loved away just as I had done.

"So what? Showing me my past isn't going to scare me."

"Pay attention," the figure chided.

Time fast-forwarded and instead of joining the police academy, I ended up falling in with Lola and her crew. I could feel the darkness taking root in this alternate version of myself. Her magic was no longer sweet and refreshing, promising a new harvest on the horizon. It was sour and bitter, full of rage and hatred for the people who had kept things from her.

Jail bars clinked shut as I saw this other version of me settle against the cold cement block wall of a prison cell. I could make out the Order's brand over my heart.

"I'd never join you. I was born to stop you from rising, remember?"

The figure reached out and touched me where the other version of me bore the brand. I gritted my teeth and tried not to flinch. "I don't think your precious ancestors foresaw the darkness that still lives inside of you. It isn't too late to align yourself with me. Together, we can bring true order to this world."

I gripped the figure's slender wrist in my right hand and shoved it away. "Go to hell, asshole!"

The figure's laughter boomed from all directions, like thunder in a raging storm. Before I realized what was happening, the sky hung above me and I lay across the stone. The figure stood above me, blade in hand. "Then you will pay the price for your refusal."

The blade plunged toward my chest and I was frozen in place, unable to stop it. And then, the figure vanished.

"Ez, we're here." Desmond's voice called to me from beyond the ether.

I blinked and sat up, my head resting in J.T.'s lap. When had I fallen over? My neck and shoulders ached from the awkward angle, the late hour, the fact my head slammed into the ground and the stress of dealing with Aoife's magic made my head throb. Looking around, I realized that we'd made it back to Dublin and our little hotel. The car idled at the front entrance. No other cars passed us as I fought to free myself from the seatbelt and climb out of the car.

"Thanks for taking us," I called to Iain through the driver-side window.

He rolled down his window. "I'm sorry I couldn't do more for you then or now. I hope you get back and are able to save your people in time. And, if you need anything more, don't hesitate to reach out to me. You've got family here. We may not be blood, but we've got a common bond." He offered his hand through the partially open window and I shook it, committing the scent of his magic to memory.

It would be good to have an ally somewhere the Order couldn't reach. I stepped back onto the sidewalk and watched him pull away. The air was chilly this late at night and I shivered in my jacket.

"Let's get inside," Des said, leading the way into the lobby of the hotel. I followed in silence with J.T. bringing up the rear. None of us spoke until the door to our room was locked securely behind us.

"This has been a crazy couple of days," J.T. said, settling into the bed we'd shared earlier.

"We need to start looking at flights home," I said, plugging my phone in and throwing myself against the pillows. I tried to sort through the dream still swirling in my mind. It had felt real—less like a dream and more like a glimpse of what was to come. Except I didn't have the power of premonition and Eleanor's magic was gone, so I couldn't be tapping into it now.

"You've got that look. What's going on in that

head of yours?" Desmond's tone was clinical, measured.

"I don't know yet. I had this weird dream when we were driving back. At least, I think it was a dream."

"Do you remember anything?" J.T. prodded, stretching out beside me.

"This cloaked figure, I couldn't see its face, attacked me. It was going to kill me if I didn't join the dark side. It showed me a messed up alternate history as if I'd joined the Order instead of finding my way back to the fold of the Authority."

"Sounds like your mind is trying to work through some emotions you maybe haven't dealt with," Desmond diagnosed.

"It felt almost like it was showing me what was coming. Though it didn't make sense. It said I would have to pay the price for not joining them and it was like I was being ... sacrificed on an altar, like what you would see in ritual depictions of the past."

"You think it has something to do with the prophecy? Like a warning?" J.T.'s eyes were fixed on mine.

I nodded, my hair rubbing against the pillow. "But, like I said, even if it was supposed to be a premonition, I don't have that power and I used the last of Eleanor's magic fighting the Order the first time. Not even Aoife had that skill." *But our blood-*

line wasn't supposed to have that trait at all. The universe has a way of ensuring the balance is kept.

Maybe this was the universe's way of making sure I didn't screw up what was coming. If Aoife was right and the balance had been out of whack for centuries, because she survived when she was supposed to die, then it was going to take a major course correction to make sure that darkness didn't descend on our world permanently.

"So, what do we do first when we get home?" Desmond's face was backlit by the glow of the computer screen.

"We need to take a head count of which families are still safe and find objects to bind their magic. I should find someplace safe to keep them, somewhere only I know."

"But shouldn't the families be able to access it? To know where this … totem is?" Des argued.

I shook my head as best I could from my position on the bed. "According to Aoife, the less people who know the location the better. It makes sense, because you limit the information getting out, fewer leaks in security."

"You said your magic has to be involved. Can't we just do it now and protect our bloodlines?" J.T. asked, reaching across me to grab pen and paper from the bedside table.

"Random objects aren't going to do it. They need to have meaning." *How do I know that?*

It would also make me feel better to do it back home where I knew my magic was strongest. Where all of our magic was rooted. My bloodline may stretch back to Ireland's ancient past, but *my* magic belonged in Boston. My home, that is where it would take root and protect my sect.

Beside me, my phone beeped with an incoming text. I snatched the phone, freeing it from the charger in one motion. Dad's name flashed on the screen and my heart skipped a beat. I opened the text to find a two-word message: call me.

My mouth went dry as I dialed his number. I tried to do the math in my head, realizing it was late on the East Coast, although not nearly as late as it was here.

"Ezri," Dad's voice was muddled by drowsiness.

"I just got your text. What's going on?"

My tone must have cleared the cobwebs, because his next words were much clearer. "Nothing's wrong, exactly. Although I did finally meet that FBI friend of yours. Molly, is it? Nice woman. She came by to check on me this afternoon."

"You worried me, Dad. You can't just send a text like that. You'll give a girl a heart attack."

"Sorry. I just wanted you to know that I'm okay and I wanted to check in on you. See how you're doing."

"We're looking at flights to come back. We have a

game plan now. Just have to hope we get back in time to fix things."

"So, you found what you were looking for then?"

"Sort of. It's probably easier if I explain when we're face to face." And cheaper. I didn't have unlimited international calling. I wanted to fill him in—a sentiment I wouldn't have had six months ago—but it was too late at night. Besides I was too tired to do it now anyways.

"If you need me to pick you up from the airport, let me know."

I shook my head even though he couldn't see it. "We'll come to you." The phone beeped in my ear with another incoming call. I checked the display to see Jacquie's number. "Dad, I need to go."

I didn't give him a chance to tell me he loved me or to say goodbye. I hung up and answered her call. "How many more have we lost?'

"I've actually got a little good news for you."

I heaved an audible sigh of relief. "Tell me."

"We managed to send an undercover cop into the pawn shop. We retrieved two necklaces."

Two was better than none. "Any luck tracking down Belladonna?"

"Not yet. We've had uniforms watching her house and Molly has some people she trusts scouring areas where her family was supposed to be located, but so far nothing."

"And you're sure she's not at home, holed up?"

"We checked."

"You physically went inside?" I prodded.

Jacquie's exhale carried with it a healthy dose of irritation. "This isn't my first time tracking down a missing person, Ezri. I know what I'm doing. So, yes, we went inside and checked. It didn't look like she'd packed a bag, but given the situation, she might have just gotten in her car and started driving."

"We have a way of returning the stolen magic and protecting the people who they haven't' gotten their hands on yet. We're coming back. Trying to catch the next flight back we can."

"Glad it wasn't a wasted trip."

"Me, too. It's been a bit rough, but worth it. See you soon."

I ended the call and focused on Desmond who still sat in front of the computer screen. "Please tell me you've got flights back booked."

"We'll land tomorrow afternoon. But we should try to grab what sleep we can. We'll need to be at the airport in about six hours."

As I crawled under the blankets, I prayed I wouldn't be plagued by bad dreams of faceless figures trying to murder me. There were only so many visions of my own death I could handle before my brain refused to function. I still had a job to do.

TWENTY-THREE

Maybe the universe was taking pity on me, because I didn't dream at all when I finally managed to fall asleep a little after four in the morning. Although that didn't mean it was a restful sleep. My body ached from unknown pains and at least twice I could dimly recall waking up to the scent of soured fruit coating me like a sugary syrup as my magic fought off some unseen foe.

I was about to start looking for a cab around five o'clock when Iain's car pulled up in front of us. "Figured you didn't need the added expense of a cabbie driving you to the airport. They charge you an arm and a leg to head that way."

Settling in the front seat again while Desmond and J.T. handled getting our bags into the back, I studied the older man's face in profile. He looked older than he had the night before. He'd dropped the glamour entirely and it appeared sustaining the car invisibility spell had really taken more out of him than I realized.

"Aoife told me that I was born to right a mistake she made," I said to fill the silence between us.

"Did she now?'

"She thinks she was supposed to die at the hands of her enemy, but her sect gave her their magic to boost hers and heal her. She thinks because that happened, this death creature that Bearach created is still around and now I have to stop it to set the balance of power right again."

"And you believe her?"

Did I? I'd seen the interaction unfold in front of my own eyes. Witnessed her be struck by Bearach's blade and the magic of those she practiced with heal her body. Her sect giving her a power boost to beat back the rising dark. However, I had no proof that she was supposed to die that day or that the balance had been shifted as a result. Just the musings of a druid who had been dead for a very long time. Finally, I answered, "I believe that she believes that's true."

"That's a very dangerous thing, believing that someone else believes in a truth. Because you can't know if they're wrong until it's too late."

"She gave me her power. I can feel it inside me. She wouldn't have done that if she didn't have some proof that she needed to set things right."

"And she expects you to take up this mantle willingly?"

"Since I was told by my mom that I was the Savior when I was eight, I've done what I had to so I could keep people safe. No, I didn't ask for this, but I took up the responsibility long before she said that magic made sure I existed. And even if she is right and the only reason I'm on this earth is to stop the bad guy she created because she lived, then so be it. I can't change that now."

"You are far more accepting of all this than I would be. It's a testament to your character, lass."

The back doors opened and closed as Desmond and J.T. climbed in. Iain pulled into the flow of morning traffic and I watched the city fall away as we neared the airport. I would miss this place, even if we'd only been here for twenty-four hours. I'd found the roots of my family and answers that I needed to save the people I cared about. It would always hold a special place in my heart.

"He's right, you are taking this better than I would have, too," Grandma said from the middle of the back seat, wedged invisibly between Desmond and J.T.

I gave her a pointed glare through the rearview mirror. I wasn't going to have a conversation with someone that only I could see in a car full of other people. I knew they wouldn't think I was crazy at this point, but it was just plain rude. She tilted her aviators down so our eyes met. "You don't have to answer, Ezzie. Just know that when the time comes, you know I'll make that sacrifice for my favorite granddaughter."

Your only granddaughter.

"Something wrong?" Desmond asked as I turned to face the back seat.

"No. Grandma just popping in to share her wisdom and support."

"That must be so disconcerting," Iain muttered.

"At least they are considerate and don't show up when I'm naked in the shower," I said with a wan smile.

"At least there's that," Des agreed. He glanced sideways at where Grandma was sitting, even though he couldn't see her. "I know you don't have many memories of her before she died, but I'd kind of wished she'd been my grandmother, too. She always made things fun and made me feel included."

"Not everyone was meant to be the hero," Grandma said softly. She patted Desmond's cheek and I swear he leaned into the gesture.

"Right, I know we've only known each other a short while, but do me a favor. Let me know you've gotten back safe," Iain said as we pulled up to the departures drop off at the airport. "And when all of this business of stolen magic and deadly children is over and done with, shoot me a message to let me know you've come through the other side" He pulled me in for a one-armed hug from the driver seat.

"I will," I said, returning the gesture.

With that, he sped off, leaving us to head inside and find our way to the terminal to make our journey home.

WE LANDED at JFK International Airport in New York at just after noon local time. I was grateful we'd been able to find a direct flight from Ireland back to the United States. We still had a two-hour layover, but it would give me time to reacclimate to East Coast time and formulate a plan of attack.

"You've got your thinking face on," J.T. teased, offering me a soda and burger.

"We don't really know if the other people's magic has been removed from those necklaces yet, do we?"

"I guess not," he answered.

Excited energy coursed through me. "So, if we can get our hands on all of them, we could restore everyone's magic and protect them from being taken again."

"Maybe. But, how are you going to figure that out? You weren't able to track them before."

"Well, we know that we're in possession of two of them. Meaning just maybe I can use them to track the others down." Desmond opened his mouth to speak, but I barreled onward. "I wouldn't go alone. And no, I wouldn't just bring mundane back-up."

"Not to poke a wound or anything, but you aren't exactly in full supply of magical allies," Desmond said.

"Let's be honest, there's no way you'd let either of us go with you," J.T. added.

"I have other people outside the Authority who have my back." Kayla and even Jonathan came to mind. Sure, I wasn't his favorite person, but I had a feeling he would take such an assault on the magical community personally. Besides, I wasn't above paying him to do a little private security work if it came to it.

I was starting to see the light at the end of this very depressing tunnel. I still had to figure out how to bind someone's magic to an object for protection, but something told me with Aoife's magic residing in the pendant, I could always call on her for some pointers. After all, putting some of a person's magical essence into the pentacle couldn't be that different. Somehow generations of my family had figured out how to do that without her help.

I sipped my soda and tried to make a game plan in my head. I'd need to let Dad know we were back without actually going to see him. I didn't know what the Order knew about my whereabouts the last couple of days, but I didn't want them to realize I'd been MIA. I would also need to gather whichever families still needed protecting and secure their magic before I went chasing down the other necklaces. Out of the corner of my eye, I caught sight of Grandma waving her aviators at me.

"I'll be right back," I announced and trekked to the nearest bathroom seven gates away. I found an empty stall and slipped inside. "What now?"

"Living in your head is an interesting place, sweetie."

I cocked my head to one side. "You're in my head?" That was new.

"We're all a part of you, remember? Anyway, I'm surprised you're not storming that sleaze ball's pawn shop demanding answers the minute you set foot back home."

"Because I don't have any reason to. No proof of anything criminal happening and that means no warrant. Without a warrant I can't just barge in there and start throwing magic around. We're going to find the other necklaces and I'm going to get those families' magic back."

"You've been saying this entire trip the Order is always ahead of you. What makes you so confident all of a sudden that things are going to turn in your favor?"

I opened my mouth to reply, but stopped. Why was I feeling so confident all of a sudden? It couldn't just be the magical boost I had in my back pocket thanks to Aoife's gift. Sure, she had great power, but I knew that once I tapped it, that would be it. Besides, that dream on the way back to Dublin hadn't been cheery. "I guess, I'm almost back home where I know the territory. It's my city. I have people there who I know have my back." Did she think I was being too overconfident?

Grandma stepped closer in the confined space of the stall and pressed her hands to my cheeks. "Just don't forget this is their home, too. I know you're strong and capable." She let go of my right cheek and tapped the center of my chest twice. "I feel it in here. And believe me, I'm thrilled you're leaning on people again. But, trusting people without magic is a dangerous proposition. They can show up with their guns and badges, but that's not going to do a bit of good when literal fire rains down around them."

"I know that, Grandma. But, like I told the guys, I'm not out of allies just yet."

"Have you thought about what you're going to do if you can't restore the magic that was taken?" She stepped back and leaned against the stall door.

"We'll just get new families on the Council. We'll make sure they're safe so the Order can't come after them for their power."

"Adding new blood changes things. Do you really want to weather that storm right before the big fight comes knocking at your door?"

"Well, no. But, what choice do I have? It's not just about people having my back. I need to have theirs, too. We need people to lead the community together."

"Just playing devil's advocate is all. Want to make sure you're truly focused on what's important."

Part of me understood her reason for poking holes in my plan. It wouldn't be a very good one if you could drive a truck through it. Even so, that tiny rebellious part of me, the teenager who'd railed against the world, hated being poked at. She despised being told she was wrong or that anyone else knew better. For a moment, I saw flashes of the alternate version of myself that the figure had showed me. Maybe it would have been easier to go down that path. *What had kept me on the side of good?*

I stared at a spot just above Grandma's left shoulder as I tried to go back over my late teenage years. It wasn't a coincidence that she was bringing it up just after that dream or warning or whatever it had been. Nothing leapt to mind. "I am focused, Grandma," I finally said. "You may think I need to just be me, but that's what I'm doing. I've always been the Savior. I've always been meant to protect people." It had carried me this far, why give up on it now?

Grandma looked like she wanted to say more, but shook her head and pointed to my pocket. "Answer your phone."

It buzzed two seconds later with an incoming text from J.T. 'Boarding now. Where are you?'

I flushed the toilet even though I hadn't used it and left the bathroom behind. I spotted Desmond and J.T. in line and wove my way through waiting passengers.

"Sorry, I'm with them," I said to a woman who glared at me when I tapped J.T. on the shoulder.

"Everything okay?" He wrapped an arm around my waist as the woman behind us huffed.

"Yeah. Guess that soda just didn't agree with me."

We handed over our boarding passes and strolled arm-in-arm down the jetway to the plane. Heading home and into the waiting arms of both friend and foe.

TWENTY-FOUR

I'd never been happier to be back home. The rumble of trains, trolleys, and cars cascaded over my ears in a beautiful cacophony. I guess I wasn't one of those people who loved to travel. I'd been away for two days and barely survived the separation anxiety. Or maybe it was that my magic missed the place where it was born.

"Where to first?" Desmond sat beside me on one of the Silver Line shuttles to South Station.

"The precinct. I need to catch up with Jacquie and Molly. See what they were able to gain from the surveillance on the pawn shop. You and J.T. should head to headquarters, start getting everyone back. As soon as we track the Order down, things are going to happen fast."

J.T. stood in front of me, holding on to one of the yellow support bars. He'd been pretty quiet since we'd gotten off the plane. I wanted to ask what was going on inside his head, but the way he kept looking around told me a very public bus wasn't the place. As the bus pulled into South Station, I stood, purposely pressing up against him.

"Whatever is bothering you, tell me."

He forced a small smile. "I'm fine. Feeling the jetlag more this direction. Go check in. We'll see you later." He kissed me on the lips and gave me a quick squeeze around the middle before we disembarked. From there we parted ways as he and Des headed for the Green Line trains and I made my way to street level. Walking to the precinct didn't sound like a bad idea.

As I headed in the direction of City Hall, I had the sense of being followed. I knew looking over my shoulder would signal to whoever was tailing me that I knew they were there. It could be an Order operative. Nailing them down here and now would only make my life easier. I stepped around a corner and waited for people to pass, putting out magical feelers to let me know of any magic that might be concealing my shadow.

An empty space in the foot traffic was my first clue that someone was shielding themselves. I could pick up a familiar scent, but with the jet lag, my brain was sluggish to make the connection. I reached out with a hand, searching for the edges of the spell and like a loose thread on a sweater, I yanked until it unraveled. I caught a fistful of shirt and pulled the person around the corner so as not to freak people out when someone randomly appeared in front of them with no explanation.

"Who are you and why are you ..." the words died on my lips as I stared at a beleaguered Belladonna. "Belladonna?" That at least answered the question of whether she still had her magic and if she was in town.

"Forgive me. I have been trying to lay low."

"No kidding. You fooled the police and FBI. They went by your place, but you weren't there."

She glanced around, obviously paranoid and with good reason. I put a gentle arm around her shoulders. "Come on. Let's grab a coffee and talk."

The precinct wasn't going anywhere and clearly Belladonna needed to talk to someone. We ended up in one of the many cafes, squirreled away in a back corner with a clear line to the exit.

"I know I should have told your partner what I was doing, but I didn't know who I could trust. If the Order is watching all of us, it is too dangerous to trust anyone."

"I understand your fear. We've lost more families from the Council. But I have a way to protect the rest of the Council's magic; at least I'm pretty sure it's going to work."

"I can't explain why but I have felt as if whoever has been watching me hasn't intended to harm me. I know it sounds foolish," she said, gripping her paper cup between her hands.

"What makes you say that?" I probed. Her spell to keep herself concealed was good, but any halfway decent practitioner would have been able to pick up on it if they knew what to look for. I had no doubt the Order operatives who were running recon weren't stupid enough to miss it.

"I saw a woman watching my building two days ago. I couldn't make out the mark, but I assumed it was there. I tried to stay away from the windows, but I needed to go out for groceries. She trailed me to the store. Even went in and bought things when I did. Then she followed me back home. But she never made any attempt to approach me."

"They were going in order of newest magic to oldest. Maybe it wasn't the right time to take yours," I proposed. Although, the fact that they'd been keeping an eye on her and attacked the Masons discredited my own words.

"Perhaps. But, from what I know of these people, they do not take failure well. Would she not have forced her way in to take what she'd come for?"

"I'm not saying there isn't something off about all this, but this entire situation is off. Like I said, I know how to stop them now. Do you think you'd feel safe enough heading back to Headquarters?"

Belladonna sipped from her cup, letting the hot coffee fortify her. "Yes. What is it you intend to do?"

"It's easier if I show you," I replied. I still hadn't exactly figured out the mechanics yet and I didn't want anyone calling me out for doing it wrong. Also I couldn't explain why, but it felt like a bad idea to share the specific need for the family object here in the open. I could tell myself it was so I only had to repeat myself once, but I knew that was bullshit. Something about the skittish look in Belladonna's eyes kept me from filling her in. "Look, I'll be there soon. I just need to check in with Jacquie and Agent Cartwright."

She gripped the coffee cup a little tighter, but nodded her head. I left her there, dialing Dad's number as I walked. The least I could do was let him know we were back. It went directly to voicemail.

"Hey Dad, it's just me. Wanted to touch base and see if we were still on for dinner tomorrow. Call me when you get this. Bye." We had no hard evidence that the Order was watching him, but I could still be careful.

"WHAT ARE YOU DOING HERE?" Molly's voice hissed in my ear the minute I stepped into view.

"Didn't Jacquie tell you I was getting back today?" I answered in confusion as she hauled me down the hallway to an interview room. She shoved me inside and pointed at the chair.

"Sit."

Caught off guard by her abrasive tone and mannerisms, I did as she instructed. I traced an old dent in the metal table with my forefinger until the door opened, both my partner and Molly reappeared.

"Please tell me there's a good reason for you hauling my ass back here like a suspect," I said.

"We told Captain Beech your assignment involved going undercover with a human trafficking ring remember? Well, she thinks you're deep under-cover, like the kind of person who wouldn't be seen strolling into a police station," Molly answered.

"Why would you tell her that?"

"Because she wanted more details than we gave. She bought it for now, but you showing up in the precinct when you're supposed to be on assignment raises all kinds of red flags," Molly answered.

"Look, I found Belladonna. Well, she found me actually. She's still in possession of her magic so either the Order got sloppy or there's still a piece to this we're missing."

"We did a little investigation of our own into your Council," Molly said, setting a manila folder down in front of me.

I flipped it open to find pictures of all the families

currently sitting on the Council with little red marks next to the families who'd lost their magic. I noted there were more than when Jacquie and I spoke last. *Damn it.* Except one thing was very obvious. Aside from Belladonna, every other family was white.

"Maybe they don't think her magic is worth taking?" Molly offered.

"Maybe. But they took three Black girls all because they might possess a power they needed." The answer felt like it should be right in front of me, but I was blind to it.

Jacquie produced an evidence bag with three necklaces inside. "We got lucky and a second undercover agent was able to snag a third one. I hope you know what you're supposed to do or who goes with which necklace."

I'd know. My ability to pick up on magical signatures hadn't failed me yet and I had to have faith it wouldn't desert me now. I thought I caught a whiff of something familiar, sweet almost, but it faded the longer my brain tried to catalog it. I took the evidence bag and stuffed it in my jacket pocket. "I'm heading over to Headquarters to fix this and protect the rest of my people. Do we have anything we can use as probable cause to scoop up Reuben?"

Jacquie and Molly exchanged looks that told me they knew something, and they didn't want to share it. "Guys come on. What is it?"

"Other than the interaction I witnessed in the pawn shop, we've got nothing," Jacquie answered.

"And Denise still won't let Neveah give a sketch even if it's through guided means?" I pressed.

"It's a no go. Denise is adamant and since Neveah is no longer in my custody, my hands are tied," Jacquie answered.

I raked my fingers through my hair. "There has to be a way we can nail this asshole."

"Like we said before unless there's some judge in the know about magic or the penal code catches up on the supernatural, our hands are tied. Retrieving a necklace from a pawn shop isn't enough," Jacquie answered.

"Do we at least know where their base of operations is?" I wasn't above paying this jackass a visit.

Jacquie put a hand on my shoulder and squeezed tight. "You go near him and I can guarantee you'll be slapped with a restraining order or accused of harassment."

"I've never even talked to him before," I protested.

"Your name has been in the paper for the kidnapping rescue. Whether you like it or not, people know who you are. At least as a cop. It didn't escape notice how young you are, either. You go knocking down this guy's door, even with what you know, and you won't be able to prove it. You'll be in no shape to protect anyone." Molly's tone was measured and calm. No doubt she'd been preparing that little speech for a while.

"Focus on what you can do right now. You have plenty of time to build a case against Reuben the right way," Jacquie added.

I exhaled long and slow to keep my temper in check. Rationally I knew they were right. At the very least I'd be risking my career if I went after him. Worse if he decided the prophecy wasn't worth waiting around to fulfill and take another swing at me. "Okay. You're right. I can at least protect the people whose magic we got back. I'll deal with the rest of it when the time comes." That time would come and soon.

"I hope you found whatever answers you needed, by the way," Molly said as she picked up the folder and opened the door.

"I did. It wasn't what I was expecting. Then again, I wasn't sure what I was expecting." I tapped the pendant through my shirt. "But I've got some extra firepower now so the Order can bring their collective asses. I'm not afraid of fighting them."

I waited until Molly had left the room before turning to my partner. She didn't look any less stressed than she had two days ago. "I'm sorry I keep dragging you into my magical messes."

She waved it off. "I signed up for this long before you crossed my path, remember? Hard to take care of two magically-inclined kids without getting messy sometimes. And believe me, I am just as frustrated as you are about not being able to nail Reuben. What he's done amounts to theft or assault. But there's no way we can convince a judge, let alone a lawyer, of that fact."

"I meant what I said, we're going to nail this bastard, not just for what he did to the Council, but for what he did to Gabby, Carly, and Neveah. He's going to pay for hurting those girls and I'm going to enjoy locking his sorry ass up."

"Go be the hero, Detective. The world needs you."

TWENTY-FIVE

As I left the precinct, a renewed sense of hope washed over me. My plan to keep J.T. and Desmond safe had worked. Sure, the Order had dealt us a heavy blow by robbing more than half of the Council of their magic, but it was one we could recover from with time and new blood. After all, magic had a way of finding a way to survive and thrive in this world. It wasn't that I planned to kick those who'd lost their magic off the Council, but other members of the community might take issue with people who could no longer practice magic leading them. Yet, we could cross that bridge when we came to it.

"Don't get cocky now," Grandma said as I made my way back to the condo to hitch a ride to Headquarters.

"I'm not being cocky. I'm being optimistic. You should try it."

She snorted. "Sweetie, I'm dead. Not a whole lot to be optimistic about."

"You know, as much as I love you, I really haven't missed you offering a nonstop commentary of my life."

She fell into step with me and wrapped an arm around my shoulders. I could almost feel the weight of it pressing down on me. "Your mother would have never forgiven me if I'd popped up when you were a teenager."

"I'm pretty sure she'd be pissed at you now." After a beat I said, "I am going to miss you when you're gone."

"I've got no plans to go anywhere, Ezzie. That part's up to you."

"I don't want to lose you, Theodora or any of the others." I pressed my palm against the pendant. "But I needed help to stop the Order the first time. And this fight that's coming, it's different, I can feel it in my bones. If that dream or vision or whatever it is, is true, then whatever Death monster Bearach unleashed is way stronger than I am on my own. It's going to take sacrificing power from people who came before me to kick it's ass."

She shrugged. "Maybe it doesn't mean all of us. And if it does, I know every one of them would gladly sacrifice what's left of their tether to this world to help you."

I arched a brow, fully realizing I looked like a crazy person talking to myself. I quickly stuck a Bluetooth headset in my ear. "Do you have pow-wows in there?"

"Where do you get these ridiculous ideas, girl? No. But, we don't have to. You're our blood, sweetheart. And we would make that ultimate sacrifice for you a thousand times over. It's what family does."

Tears came unbidden to my eyes and I wiped them away with the back of my hand. Her words conjured images of my mother's death and I did not need to go down that rabbit hole now. Not when I had people counting on me.

"Do me a favor, Grandma, and lay low for a while. I'm going to need to concentrate to restore the magic in these necklaces. No offense, but you're distracting as hell."

Grandma leaned in and kissed my cheek. "You got it. But, remember, I'm not far if you need me."

I know.

J.T. stood outside the building looking at his phone. I nudged his shoulder and he jumped, his lips turning into a smile when he saw me.

"Everything go okay at the precinct?"

I patted my pocket. "I've got the necklaces. And Belladonna is okay. She was using her magic to hide herself. But she swore she'd be there at Headquarters."

"Good. Des and I were talking. We think we've got some objects we can use to bind our family magic."

"Good. We should get going then. The sooner everyone is protected, the better."

He slid into the driver seat and I settled in the passenger seat. He reached over and squeezed my left hand, his thumb running across my knuckles, stopping on my ring finger.

"I wish you didn't have to be the one people keep making prophecies about," he sighed and started the engine.

"If you believe Aoife, I was literally made to fulfill the first one." It still sounded insane when I said it out loud. Yet, instinctually, I also knew it made sense. The world needed balance. I'd felt what it was like when the scales were tipped for the worse.

"I'm worried I'm going to lose you to this fight, Ez."

I turned to study his profile. "Where's this coming from? I'm fine. We're all going to be fine."

"I want to believe that. But people have died because of this fight before and I don't want it to be you."

"Hey, I've said I'm going to be okay. I've beaten them before and with Aoife's added power boost, it's going to be enough to stop them."

He chewed his lower lip in silence as the highway passed us by. I understood his fears. I'd be a liar if I didn't share them. Despite that I needed to put my fear aside, bury it deep because people were counting on me and needed me to have my shit together. So, I'd be afraid when all of this was over.

The circular driveway was crammed with cars as we pulled up. I hoped they hadn't gathered spectators. I squared my shoulders and marched up the steps. Inside the foyer was empty, but I could hear voices coming from the floor above. I took the stairs two at a time and burst through the meeting room doors to find everyone had gathered. Avery was firmly attached to Desmond's arm—no doubt grateful to have her husband back where she could keep tabs on him—and I spotted Belladonna in the corner, apart from everyone else.

"First, I want to say thank you for coming in. I know we told you staying home was safer. But we've got some new information and I'm going to fix what I can," I began.

"What does that mean?" A chorus of voices asked.

I pulled out the evidence bag with the three necklaces. "We were able to retrieve three of the containers. I know that isn't everyone's magic and I'm sorry but at this point, we have to assume it's gone." Without being able to track down the Order's base of operations, there was little chance we could retrieve those necklaces. Besides I doubted the Order would have waited to transfer the magic within them.

"Gone?" Richard bellowed. "It can't just be gone!"

"How do we decide who gets that magic, then?" Belladonna's voice was low.

"We don't," I answered. "It belongs to a particular person. I'm going to figure out who and return it." I held up a hand to call for silence. "For those of you whose magic hasn't been touched, I also have a safeguard. I'm going to need you to bring me an object that has particular sentimental meaning to your family."

"What will that do?" Desmond voiced, even though I'd already explained it to him.

"We're going to bind the family's magic to this object so it can't be taken away. Then I'm going to secure the objects somewhere only I know. That way, none of you could be forced to reveal the location."

I needed to figure out whose magic resided in each necklace. Aoife had said I would know how to tell, and I had to trust that she was right. I took the first necklace from the bag and it pulsed bright purple in my hand. By the look of expectant faces, I couldn't tell if they saw the essence of the magic or not. The stress of travel and unravelling Belladonna's spell clogged my senses. I had to re-center myself with the sandalwood charm. The room snapped into focus as the necklace continued to pulsate. I could almost feel it searching for its rightful place.

I wasn't sure at first what to expect. Would it leap from the necklace and hover over the correct person? Or would it be more subtle? Ultimately, it was a mixture of the two. Pale purple light shimmered in the air, dancing along dust particles until it wrapped itself around a woman's neck like a kerchief.

"Here. Hold this," I told her and passed the necklace to her.

The second necklace strobed wild pulses of orange light, like it had caught the afternoon sunlight. I thought I picked up on a faint shimmer leading me to the second recipient, but he frowned and said, "I still have my magic."

I gave an embarrassed nod and focused again. I put out into the world that I needed it to guide me just a little. It wasn't a laser beam, but when I opened my eyes a very clear connection existed between the jewelry in my hand and Shawna sitting at the end of the semi-circle. I passed her the necklace.

The last one thrummed against my palm, emitting green vapors. They rose from the necklace and disappeared into the air. No connection appeared like it had with the other two. I took another deep breath and poured more of my own power into the spell. *Show me where you belong.*

Tiny green vine-like shoots erupted from the heart of the necklace and wound their way down my fingers, to the floor and slithered all the way to the middle-aged man sitting in the middle of the semi-circle. I handed him the necklace and the vines vanished. Or maybe they hadn't really been there at all.

"And what about the rest of us? What are we supposed to do?" Richard's voice carried a sharp edge of defeat and anger.

I swallowed the lump in my throat and answered in as authoritative a tone as I could muster. "I'm going to need all the families who were affected to go through the rolls and choose successors to the Council."

"You're just removing us like we never existed?" He scoffed.

"We've never had people without active magical abilities on the Council. If we can't show that we can collectively safeguard the community, they'll lose faith in us," I replied.

"And seeking replacements shows strength?" He sighed.

"It shows that you are willing to accept a change in circumstance. You're not being booted from the community. You have years of knowledge that we need. That the next generation needs to learn. But, practically speaking, we need people who can do magic leading us "

He huffed, but stood and led the other members who'd been affected out of the room. Belladonna shuffled forward. "I'll have to go home and gather something for this binding spell."

"Of course. But, do me a favor and text me when you get there and when you are coming back. Your cloaking spell was good, but we know they're watching us."

She gave my shoulder a half-hearted pat before leaving the room. I faced three people I'd only just gotten to know along with J.T., Avery, and Desmond. At least it made it easier to figure out which magic went with each person. Time to improvise.

"I'm going to need a large space to work so it's probably better if you three wait outside. I can't risk your magic getting in the way. I promise, I'll send someone to get you if I need you."

J.T. kissed my cheek. "Be safe."

"I totally have this room wired with mics and cameras," Avery said in passing as she led the guys out of the room.

That should have filled me with unease, but I found it oddly comforting. That still left me alone with three people who were counting on me.

"Okay, bear with me. I haven't exactly done this

before." *Ever.* "Can any of you feel your magic calling out to you?"

The three of them glanced around, down at the necklaces and back to me. "No," the middle-aged man answered. What was his name again? Albert?

"It's there and it wants to be back inside you," I said.

"How do you know?" Shawna asked, her hand resting against her belly. At least it seemed she and her baby were still okay.

"It's going to sound bizarre, but I could kind of see your magic. It is still linked to you, because there's still a part of you that is inherently magical. Magic is like energy; it can't really be destroyed. Just transferred around." I pointed to Albert. "Tell me, what does your magic smell like?"

"Uh, pine trees."

I inhaled, focusing on the necklace in his hand. Pine, like air fresheners, hit me. His brow furrowed as he looked around. "I ... I can smell it."

"Shawna, what about you?"

"Grapefruit," she answered immediately.

The scent of pine was still strong in my nose, but I could pick up the citrus smell of her magic and it left an odd taste on my tongue. Her eyes lit up as she, too, picked up on the scent.

"What about you?" I turned to the last woman.

"Lilies."

Then just like what had happened with Shawna

and Albert, the heady floral scent joined the mixture. Her eyes welled with tears. "I can't feel it though," she said, wiping at her eyes.

"That's the last part," I said, praying I was right.

"You must guide the magic back. It needs to know where to go," Theodora's voice was gentle in my ear.

I managed not to flinch at the sudden addition to the conversation, but I was grateful to have her guiding me. I turned my back to the three people sitting before me, hoping to keep the questions I had to myself.

"How do I do that?" I barely moved my lips.

"Call the magic residing in each vessel to you, it will obey. It wants to be directed. The recipient must be willing. That should not be difficult as the magic is meant for them. It belongs there."

"Is everything okay?" Shawna interrupted.

I spun around faster than necessary. "Yes. Sorry, just need to make sure I'm in the ... uh, right head-space to do this. It's a very delicate spell and I want to get it right."

"And here you said you'd never done it before," Albert grumbled.

"All the more reason she should take her time and be sure of what she's doing," Shawna snapped at him, rubbing her belly again.

As much as I wanted to get Shawna and her baby on their way, I knew it wasn't right to do the first test on her in case something went wrong. I stepped up to Albert and took the necklace back. Theodora gave me an encouraging nod. *Here goes nothing.* I held the necklace in my left hand with my right cupped beneath it. I squinted, feeling the energy and magic around me crackling over my skin. Like little jolts of electricity, begging to be used. I let the reassuring scent of my own magic build up around me, encasing me in a bubble of protection. If this went sideways, I needed to have a way to protect the people sitting in front of me. Slowly, the puffs of green energy coming from the necklace slowed and started dripping out of the necklace to pool in my cupped palm. The fresh scent of pine mingled with the earthiness of my strawberry as the magic sought out a place to connect.

I stepped toward Albert, guiding the magic back to him. "Come on. You've got this," I muttered to myself. The green pool turned thicker the closer I got to Albert and I took it as a good sign that the magic recognized its rightful host.

"Albert, I need you to hold out your hands, palms up."

He did as instructed and I tipped my hand over, letting the magic drip onto his skin. I wasn't sure what I expected to happen when it made contact, but the explosion of forest smell knocked me back a few steps. It sprouted like vines and wrapped itself around his forearms. Albert's eyes went wide as the vines continued up his arms and across his chest, settling together over his heart. He inhaled sharply as the vines disappeared.

"I can feel it again," he breathed.

"Test it out," I prompted.

He stood up and with a minor wave of his hand, I could feel the energy in the room shift as the chair he'd vacated tipped backward onto its back two legs before spinning in a circle.

"Thank you," he said, wrapping me in an unexpected hug.

"Sure. Now, go get something that holds meaning for your family so we can make sure no one can take it away again," I said.

He darted from the room and I turned to Elaine. Shawna sat quietly, patiently waiting. I needed one more test to make sure I didn't screw it up for her and her baby. So, taking the second necklace back, I let the magic pool in my hand before releasing it back. It melted into her palms, but I could see tiny vapors as it travelled up her torso and settled again over her heart. She turned and with a whoosh of floral scent, the curtains zipped shut.

Then it was Shawna and me. I sat beside her and put a hand on her shoulder. "You ready to have this back where it belongs?"

She nodded. "Since it happened the baby hasn't been moving much. The doctor said she's fine, but it's like she knows something's missing."

"Well, we're going to get this magic back inside you and hopefully that makes your baby kick for days."

She smiled and passed the necklace back. By the third time, my magic didn't even need instruction on what I wanted. It just did it, pulling the captive magic into my hand before I passed it back to Shawna. Instead of racing to her heart, it branched, wrapping around her belly before disappearing. I was about to ask her to test her magic when she gave a small gasp and pressed her hand to her side.

"I can feel her again. Thank you."

"I'm just sorry I couldn't return everyone's magic."

"I know I'm probably biased, but you are only one person. You aren't super-human, no matter what people might think. People seem to forget how young you are, too. You've got so much responsibility riding on your shoulders; I can't imagine how you handle it all."

"I haven't really had a choice." There was a time not long after my mother's death that I wondered what it would have been like if I'd never been born with magic or if someone else was the Savior. I'd still have a mother. Maybe I would have gone off to college somewhere else and become a lawyer. I turned my attention back to Shawna. "I know there's going to be pain and tension when we transition new Council members in. People are going to want to know why and how we're going to keep them safe. Honestly, I'm not sure what to tell them."

"That you are doing everything in your power to be the leader that they need, but it takes more than one person to create a good defense."

"Thanks."

Shawna pushed herself to her feet and left me alone in the meeting room. The lingering mixture of magic made me dizzy and sort of sleepy. Or maybe it was the jet lag. My eyelids grew heavy and I felt my head loll to one side.

A strong wind whipped around me, tugging at my hair and my clothes. It wanted to rip me apart. Thick clouds swirled overhead and funneled toward my feet like a tornado touching down. I took a step back, unsure of what would emerge until that same shrouded figure appeared.

"This again? Look, I get it. You think I should have joined you and I didn't. You can't change history."

"You believe you have dealt me a great blow, cutting off the source of my nourishment," it said.

Could it feel that I'd returned the magic? Did it know what I was planning to do next? "Guess your lackeys should have been faster."

"I am strong enough to do what must be done, child of my enemy."

"You know, if you're that eager to get your ass

kicked, we could skip this whole prophecy business and just do it right now. Name a place, I'll be there."

The figure shook its head, sending peals of ghoulish laughter into the air. "Do not be so eager to meet your end, Savior. You are not yet ready for our final meeting, but you will be, soon."

The figure vanished and I sat up, confused by my surroundings. How long had I been asleep? J.T stood over me, worry lines etched into his face. "You were talking in your sleep."

"Sorry. Just a weird dream," I mumbled, rubbing at my forehead.

"No, it wasn't. I saw you on that car ride back to Dublin, Ez. That wasn't a dream then and it wasn't one now. What is going on?"

"Honestly, I'm not sure, but I think whatever it is I'm supposed to stop in December, this Death's child thing, it can get in my head. Connect with me somehow and it's taunting me. It knows I returned the magic."

"How could it possibly know that?"

"I don't know, but it specifically mentioned cutting off its food supply."

He pulled me into a tight hug until I could hear his heartbeat resounding in my ear like a steady drum. The rhythm telling me that even if I'd failed some people, I still had him. No matter what had gone down in our past, he was here for me—flaws and all.

"I love you," I whispered into the fabric of his t-shirt.

"I love you, too." He gave me a squeeze and leaned back. "Your job isn't done."

Time to see if I was as good as my ancestors in using binding magic.

I stood outside the door to the library on the first floor, listening to the low murmur of voices from inside. I knew I needed to go in and finish what I'd set out to do. Even so it still scared me. Returning three council members magic had been one thing, but that was taking it from somewhere it shouldn't be and sending it back where it belonged. This felt different. In that moment, I longed to hear my mother's voice giving me direction and guidance.

"I am not your mother, but I believe I can aid you," Theodora said from beside me.

"I'll take anything you've got," I said.

"You must first remember that binding magic to a physical object requires a willing relinquishment of that magic."

"Voluntary. Okay. That makes sense. But Aoife

said my magic had to be involved. Couldn't they just use their own intent to bind it?"

"You are not merely binding one person's magic, but an entire bloodline. From what I understand, you are there to bind the whole of the magic. You have consent of one, but you are swearing to guard all who follow and who have come before."

"More responsibilities," I muttered.

"Yet one that is no different than what you have already sworn to do as a member of this Council and as an enforcer of the law," she noted.

I let her words sink in. Making the promise to protect future generations wasn't that different from sitting on the Council and helping to shape the magical community. Sure, my position as a police officer was wider ranging but that, too, meant I was offering people protection from harm.

"Okay," I said, grasping the door handle "Let's do this.'

The room fell silent as I walked in. It hurt not to see everyone I'd become accustomed to seeing sitting at the table. My phone buzzed in my pocket as I studied the faces waiting for me. Belladonna wasn't among them. My phone buzzed a second time, almost as if it became more insistent the longer I ignored it. Albert cleared his throat. I took a step back and turned to pull out my phone, half-expecting Dad to be leaving a rambling voicemail in response to my cryptic call. It was a simple text from Belladonna telling me she was on her way back. A knot between my shoulders loosened just a touch.

"Okay, so, I know this whole situation sucks big time and you're all probably wondering how I'm going to keep your family's magic safe," I said, hoping that voicing my own fears would help keep everyone calm. "But this is going to work."

"Do you know why they attacked us like this?" Shawna asked from the seat closest to me on the righthand side of the table.

"Most of you know about the latest prophecy that Nevaeh DeWitt had." A sea of faces nodded back at me. "From what I've been able to learn, they are trying to amass as much power as they can to try and take me out. Raising ancient druids wasn't enough and they know that. So, they're trying to take away anyone who can help me fight back. I really am sorry you all got pulled into this bullshit."

My cheeks flushed a little as the word slipped out. No doubt some of them were judging me for my word choice. Shawna reached over and patted my hand like she'd done upstairs. "We accepted being part of this bullshit along with you when we decided that fighting the good fight was worth it. We have your back no matter what."

Her confidence washed over me, along with a hint of her magic and I smiled back at her. "Okay, let's get started. You're going to need to voluntarily link your magic to these items and you have to remember that it's not just your magic you're locking in. It's your ancestors who came before you and everyone, of your blood who comes after."

Murmurs of assent went up around the room just as the door behind me opened and Belladonna slipped in, looking harried. J.T. was out of his seat at the back of the room and shoving a glass of water into her hand before I could ask if she was all right. He could have manifested the glass for all I knew. I let him guide her back to where he'd been sitting as I took a seat beside Shawna.

"It has been in my family for generations," she explained, presenting a war medal.

I laid it across my left hand and my entire body jumped to attention as if hooked up to a generator. It wasn't the same sense as when I touched my own pendant, but somehow I could still feel the chain of magic, going back through her family line. It was strong and it would do just fine to keep her family's lineage protected.

"Okay, so, I need you to pour some of your magic into it with the explicit intent of keeping it safe within the medal," I instructed, praying that what I was saying would work and that I was somehow channeling Aoife's knowledge.

"I'll try," Shawna whispered. She placed her

hand on top of the medal and her magic erupted around us. I could see the tendrils of it racing from each fingertip to secure itself around the medal in my hand.

"You will need a small sacrifice to secure the binding," Theodora's voice whispered in my ear.

I opened my mouth to ask what she was talking about when she manifested a pin and pricked my finger, letting the blood bubble onto the pad of my finger. *Wonderful, more bleeding.* The tiniest hint of strawberry leeched into the air to mix with Shawna's own citrus scent. The tendrils of magic linking Shawna to the medal snapped and she slumped back against the chair.

"Did it work?" She asked, winded.

I could see the combination of our magic sinking into the hammered finish of the medal. "It worked," I assured her.

One down, only a few more to go. I lost track as my magic mingled with so many other people's that I wondered if I'd be able to tell my own from the rest ever again.

"You should take a break," Desmond said from beside me.

I shook my head and wiped the drowsy feeling from my eyes. "I'm almost done. Just you, J.T., and Belladonna left. It's safer to finish now."

"It is safer for you to rest and not overexert yourself if you are to be of any use to the rest of us in the time to come," Belladonna said, her tone the most authoritative I'd heard from her in months.

"Come on, let's get some food in you," J.T. said. Without giving me a chance to argue, he hoisted me out of the chair and down the hallway to the kitchen. He pointed to the table and benches where I'd first met Belladonna. I sat down. He busied himself with making me what I guessed were sandwiches by the way he rummaged through the cupboards for bread and the fridge for meat and cheese.

"Did you let your dad know we were back?" He asked without looking up from his food prep.

"I left him a message. He hasn't called back." I pushed the nugget of worry in my stomach down.

"At least he knows when he gets the message," J.T. muttered.

"What's going on? You're acting weird," I said.

He looked over his shoulder and for a split second he was the fresh-faced teenager who'd stolen my heart. He'd been a shameless flirt back when we first met, but I'd been starstruck the moment I met him. I'd be lying if I said I hadn't hated myself and regretted pushing him away for ten years.

"I'm not acting weird," he proclaimed.

"Yes, you are. You've been quiet and kind of off since we left Dublin. What is going on?'

He set a plate of sandwiches in front of me and

sat down with his back to the table. "I've just been thinking about things."

"What sort of things?" I took a sandwich and bit in. Ham, provolone and just a touch of mayo, exactly the way I liked it.

He studied his hands which were balled into fists in his lap. "The past, the future. Us."

I swallowed. "Vague much?"

He turned so we were face to face. "Ezri, you know I love you, right?"

"Of course, I do. What's going on? You're starting to freak me out."

He licked his lips and looked down at his hands. I caught movement, like he was passing something small from palm to palm. My heart sped up making my chest ache. My brain shouted at me, warning what was coming. Although it didn't convey my surprise when he pushed himself off the bench to land on one knee, a simple silver ring in his right hand.

"I know we've only been back together for a few months and that we just moved in together but Ez, it's always been you. I was hurt when you lashed out and cut yourself off, but I understood you were grieving. And I believed it when people told me you'd come back to us."

He must mean someone like Desmond, who knew the truth about my mother's sacrifice. "J.T. we talked about this."

"I know, and the timing was off. It came across like I was jumping on Desmond's bandwagon, but I wasn't. I wanted to ask you while we were in Dublin, but everything got so crazy. I know you're worried about not having allies in the fight to come. But I want you to know that you'll always have me. I want to be your partner in this and in life. Ezri Ann Trenton, will you marry me?"

My mouth went dry and my hands grew slick with sweat. The bite of sandwich swirled uncomfortably in my stomach as I studied my boyfriend's face and the tiny ring in his hand. It was simple and just what I would want. I did love him, but it felt like he was asking because our future was so uncertain. I needed him in my life and telling him no would ruin what we had.

"On one condition," I said.

His eyes lit up and he leaned forward. "Anything."

"We wait to get married until this thing with the Order is finished. I need something to look forward to."

He wrapped his arms around my neck and pulled me in for a lingering kiss that made the nerves and the sloshing of my stomach vanish. I snaked my arms around his torso and held on tight. Out of the corner of my eye, I saw Grandma standing there with her aviators in one hand, a broad grin on her face.

"I told you he was worth keeping around."

I let out a small laugh before pulling back and awkwardly giving J.T. my hand. "Well, go on. You better make this thing official before the world ends."

He slid the ring on my finger and kissed me again. I expected the added weight of the ring to throw me, but it felt as if it had always been there. I hoped that was a sign of good things to come.

TWENTY-SEVEN

We returned to the library to find Desmond sitting alone. I looked around in confusion. "Where's Belladonna?"

"She said she didn't think she needed the protection after all," he answered.

"No, just because they didn't get to her yet doesn't mean they won't take a swing at her when we aren't looking or when she lets her guard down."

"I told her as much, but she was insistent that she was going to get out of town for a while. She said she's the last living member of her family, but she's got friends out of state she can stay with for a while. Something about a ranch in North Dakota or something."

That didn't sit well with me. Why had she come back if she was just going to take off again? J.T. pressed the palm of his hand into my back, guiding me to the chair beside my cousin. "I might as well do the binding spell with the two of you then."

Desmond produced something in a small square box. He opened it to reveal a prayer medallion I hadn't seen in years. It had come from his dad's side of the family and had been passed down from father to son on their thirteenth birthday. Desmond had been so proud to receive it, showing it off to everyone who'd listen, myself included. It wasn't inherently magical, but it was just as much a part of Desmond's lineage. I took it gently between my fingers. The metal thrummed against my skin. Not in the same way that Shawna's medal had, but I could still read the familial connection tracing back through his mortal bloodline.

"What made you pick this? Why not something from your mom's side of the family?'

He gave me one of his trademark arched brows. "Did you forget that you inherited all the cool family heirlooms from the magical side of the bloodline?"

"Is it going to be strong enough?" J.T. interjected.

"I think so." Only one way to know for sure.

"Focus on pouring a little of your magic into it," I instructed.

"I heard the spiel the last four times you did it, Ez."

I barely avoided rolling my eyes as he acted like the know-it-all older cousin that he was. He placed his hand on top of mine and spearmint tickled my nose making my lips tingle. I expected him to give up more than the trickle that was coming from him, but maybe he thought our bloodlines were so close that giving too much would screw up the spell. The little spot on my finger welled up like it had a mind of its own and my fruity scent mixed with Desmond's magic to lock around the medallion.

"You're good," I said and set the medallion with the other items. All that remained was J.T.

He switched spots with Desmond and held out an engraved placard with the Hippocratic Oath inscribed on it. I still remembered the day he'd shown it to me and said it would be passed on to him from his mom when he officially started medical training. I hadn't been around when she'd actually passed it on. Cupping the placard in both hands, he laid his hands on top of mine and honey erupted in the room as he poured his intent into the item. The promise of what his family's magic had been and what it could still be in the future—our future. My own magic rose up to meet him, winding into the tiny spaces between his essence, as if to say, "this is where I belong."

The mixture died down and he leaned over to kiss me. "I love you."

"I love you, too," I repeated, a blush creeping up my cheeks as Desmond stood nearby trying to act like he hadn't just seen us.

"What are you going to do now?" J.T. prodded as I set his placard with the others.

"Find somewhere safe and secure to keep these where the Order can't get their hands on it."

"I'm guessing the back of the closet at home isn't in the running?" He grinned, and it made his eyes light up.

"Sadly, no." I did have one idea. "I'll take care of it." I turned to Desmond. "I may actually need your help."

"I thought this was supposed to be somewhere only you know."

"If I need a back-up, you're the person I'd want to know the information."

"Let me go tell Avery that I'll be late for dinner."

He darted from the library leaving J.T. and I alone. He took my left hand in his right, rubbing his thumb over the ring that now adorned it. "So, you going to tell your dad at least?"

"You're telling me he doesn't already know?"

"I may have floated the idea before we moved in together. He didn't object."

"Yes, I'll tell him." My phone buzzed with an incoming call in my pocket with dad's ringtone. "Speak of the devil."

I stepped into the hallway. "Hey, Dad."

"Hi, sorry I missed your call earlier. I was at the movies and then I forgot to turn my phone back on. Everything okay?"

"We're fine. Did what we could to stop these assholes from stealing more magic. And now I just have to find a way to build a case against the bastard who is behind all of this."

"Be careful. You may have magical powers and may be a cop, but you're still my little girl."

"I know, Dad. I will be careful. Look, thanks for touching base. I need to go. Des and I have an errand to run. Then, you, J.T., and I should grab dinner."

"Oh, fancy. What are we celebrating?"

I couldn't hide the smile that leapt to my face. "I promise to tell you at dinner. Bye."

Desmond reappeared at the bottom of the stairs and gestured to the front of the building. "Shall we?"

I scooped up my bizarre little treasure trove and we headed out into the fall afternoon. It had gotten chilly since I'd come inside. I followed Des to his little BMW and slid into the passenger seat.

"You want to drive?" He offered.

"No. I just need to get to any bank with safety deposit boxes."

"Good thinking, but why not a bank you already have an account with?"

"Too easy for them to track."

The strands of magic protecting the items in my lap clogged up my nose, making me sneeze. As I leaned back, I caught Desmond's gaze following my left hand.

"Don't tell me you didn't know about this," I said.

He shook his head. "Not a thing. But I take it congratulations are in order?"

"Thanks. I guess he'd been planning it for a while, and he was worried you and Avery stole his thunder."

"In hindsight, we probably should have told close friends and family what was happening. You don't look as excited as I thought you would be."

I spun the ring around on my finger. "I am. But I told him we should wait until everything with the Order is over. I want to have something to look forward to, you know?"

"You both deserve to be happy, Ez, but if this year has proven anything, things with the Order may never be over. Cling to that happiness and bright spot while you can."

"Maybe we'll just do what you guys did. I never really wanted a big church wedding." That was a lie since I'd dreamed of it as a little girl. I'd even spent afternoons imagining what my wedding would be like when J.T. and I first started dating. Though with my mother gone, I couldn't handle having a big to do without her there.

I checked my phone, realizing I hadn't let Iain know we'd gotten back without a problem. I bit my lip as I dialed the international number he'd given me.

"Yeah?" Iain's voice came through the line after the first ring.

"Um, Iain, hi, it's Ezri. I just wanted to let you know we got back safely and took care of everything we'd talked about."

"Oh, brilliant, lass. Good to hear it."

"Will this do?" Desmond interrupted the conversation and pointed up at one of the many banks in the city.

"Sure, Des ..." I said, "Iain, sorry to make this so quick, but I've got an errand that needs to be done."

"You take care now."

I ended the call and Desmond pulled into a metered spot. Together we headed inside, approaching the teller at the far end of the counter.

"Good afternoon, how can I help you today?" Her overly cheery high-pitched voice and wide smile felt forced.

"I need to rent a safety deposit box," I answered and patted the bag of items on the counter beside me.

"Certainly." She tapped away at her computer. "Do you have an account with us already?"

"I don't," I replied.

"I see." She pressed her lips into a thin line. "I'll need my manager's approval to start the process then. Give me just a minute."

The teller disappeared into the back of the bank for a few minutes and I closed my eyes, drumming my fingers on the counter. Was it that complicated to get her manager's approval?

"Miss, if you'd come with us, we'll get you set up," the teller said.

I opened my eyes to see her wave us around the side of the counter. I felt safer having Desmond at my back as we followed the woman down a short hallway and into a room lined with long rectangular boxes. She produced two keys and inserted them into a box near the bottom on the far-left wall. She slid the box free from its place and set it on the table in the center of the room before passing over some paperwork.

"I'll just need you to fill this out. Once you've done that, you can take the first key and return the second to my manager across the hall."

"Thanks."

She eased the door partially shut behind her, leaving Desmond and I inside. I set the bag of items in the box and filled out the information on the form, signing my name at the bottom with a flourish.

"Let's get out of here. This place is starting to give me a really bad feeling," I said.

I left the second key and form with the manager as instructed before tucking my key in the inner zipper pocket of my jacket. The teller gave us a little wave as we left the lobby and headed back toward Desmond's car.

Sunlight glinting off a building across the way temporarily blinded me. As I raised my hand to block the light, I felt something bump my shoulder, sending me staggering sideways as a sound like a sack of potatoes hitting the ground ricocheted in my ears.

"What the hell was that?" I turned, expecting Desmond to answer. Instead, to find him sprawled on the sidewalk, a neat little bullet wound in his chest. "Desmond!"

Everything slowed to a painful crawl as I stared down at my cousin. *Had he pushed me out of the way? Was that bullet meant for me?* I fell to my knees and pressed a hand against his chest, fumbling for my phone with the other, slamming my finger against the Home button until it prompted me as to whether this was an emergency. "Hang on, help is coming," I said to Des as my phone connected with 9-1-1.

"9-1-1, what is your emergency?" A calm male voice said on the other end of the line.

"This is Detective Ezri Trenton, Major Crimes. I need an ambulance. I've got a man down. Gunshot wound to the upper left chest," I said, trying to take in all of the details. My brain couldn't be bothered to remember if I was still supposed to be undercover or not.

"Stay on the line, Detective. I'm tracking your location," the operator said, still exhibiting calmness that I had to believe was drilled into them in training. Even so, it did nothing to ease my own frantic nerves.

I set the phone on the sidewalk beside me and scooted around to hold Desmond's head in my lap.

His chest was barely moving beneath my hand. "Hang in there."

"I can ... feel it," he rasped.

Trying to recall the position he'd been standing when he was hit, I looked over my shoulder. I didn't see anything that would indicate an exit wound. "It's probably still in there. You need to be still until the paramedics get here."

"Burning. Like fire," he answered, reaching up with his right hand to hold tight to my wrist.

"I know it hurts." Tears began to stream down my cheeks, blurring my vision. Not enough to hide the red spreading across my hands and his shirt.

I didn't notice if a crowd had begun to gather until a shadow fell across Desmond's legs. None of that mattered. Only that someone had taken a shot at my family. Desmond's grip on my wrist tightened as his body seized.

"They're almost here, Des. Just hang on a little longer. Everything's going to be okay."

"I'm sorry I didn't tell you before," he said, blood frothing on his lips.

"Shut up and save your breath." I leaned over, the pendant around my neck brushing against his chest. "And I know you're sorry."

"Saw it coming," he coughed.

"You're not making sense," I whispered, stroking his hair, trying to keep the pressure on the wound.

His hand latched on to the pendant and his grip

nearly choked me as he held on with whatever strength he had left. All around me, spearmint puffed in thick clouds. Or at least that's what they would have been if they'd been visible to non-practitioners. My brain was too slow to catch up to what Desmond was doing. He wouldn't do what I thought he was doing. He didn't know *how*.

"No, stop," I protested, but it was too late. His magic faded and the pendant around my neck grew white-hot with his magic as it seeped into the metal and the pink-tinged diamond at its heart. My cousin's magic, what was left of it, was now locked inside my pendant.

A flurry of movement passed through my peripheral vision as the paramedics arrived, urging me out of the way so they could work. I slumped back on the sidewalk, watching, but not really taking in the scene before me as they searched for a pulse, tried to administer CPR. None of it mattered, because all of his magic had left him and was now neatly secured in the family heirloom only I'd been given. I really was the last of Harrow's blood now.

I fingered the pendant with my non-bloody hand as tears streamed down my cheeks and a realization hit. The magic held there wouldn't be any use to Desmond now anyway.

SEPTEMBER 22, 2017

TWENTY-EIGHT

Twenty-four hours wasn't enough time to process that he was *gone*. The paramedics had pronounced him dead at the scene. I'd scrubbed my hands a dozen times since then. Despite that I could still see his blood on my skin, still feel the slickness of it between my fingers, sticking to everything I touched.

His dad had insisted we hold a small ceremony to say goodbye, even though the medical examiner wouldn't release his body for weeks. Guilt and anger weighed on me as I stood in the back garden at head-quarters. Cool autumn air swirled around me, sending shivers through my body. I glanced around at the small group assembled—J.T., my dad, Avery, and Desmond's dad—and another wave of anger crashed over me. This shouldn't be happening. Not now, not ever. At least his mom didn't have to carry the pain of burying her son. She'd died of breast cancer six years ago. I'd been so consumed in my own anger I hadn't even gone to the funeral.

"I never thought we would be having this ceremony," his dad said, dabbing at his eyes with a tissue. This family had endured so much loss already. "But I know he wouldn't have wanted a big to-do."

"I know this is what he would want," Avery said in a soft tone, reaching out to pat her father-in-law's shoulder.

"He'd want to be alive," I muttered loud enough for my words to carry.

No one spoke in response to my outburst, not that I expected anyone to scold me. The air between us grew thick with unspoken grief and I tried my best to push all of the pain down for just a few minutes. To send Desmond off like he deserved. Even if I knew a part of him still remained in the pendant, stubbornly refusing to come out and tell me everything was going to be okay.

Those of us with magic stepped forward and joined hands. I felt J.T. grip my left hand tight as we all closed our eyes. The wind died down in the center of our circle and I could swear the faintest hint of spearmint wafted around me, winding through my senses. It brought fresh tears to my eyes. When no one else spoke, I exhaled and opened my mouth.

"Desmond, your spirit has left this realm and

gone on to the next. But your magic remains a part of each within this circle. Your blood and those with whom you bonded in life carry you onward. Rest now, kin."

My voice hitched on the last word and I broke the circle. Swallowing back a sob as I raced back inside, winding my way to the council meeting room. The community had given us space to hold our ritual. I needed space away from everyone and no one else was occupying it.

"Let it all out, Ezzie," Grandma said, her hand almost pressing against my back in a show of support.

"I don't want to talk to *you*," I snapped.

"Tough shit, kid. Life ain't fair. I know you want to see him, but he's not ready to see you. Not yet."

"But I need him."

"You need to get your head on straight. We both know you're sliding into that darkness and something tells me he's not coming out until you have it under control."

The bluster went out of me and I sunk onto the nearest chair, burying my head in my hands. "I failed him."

"Oh, now stop that right now. You failed no one."

"He's dead ... because of me. If we hadn't been so connected, he wouldn't have been there and he'd still be alive."

"Last I checked neither of you had the gift of foresight. So, enough with the self-blame."

"I feel so lost without him," I whispered. Ironic given how hard I'd pushed him away for so long. Now I couldn't imagine my life without him, but that was the reality I now faced.

"Lean on the ones left behind. All of you are going through the same pain. And when the time is right, you'll know when it is, he'll come back to you." She brushed her thumbs across my cheeks, attempting to wipe away the tears.

She vanished, leaving me alone in the space. Beyond, I heard low voices and then footsteps on the staircase. The scent of food wafted through the open door, but I ignored it. I wasn't interested in any more socializing, not even when J.T. appeared in the doorway, worry lines creasing his forehead.

"You need to eat something," he said, trying to push something into my hand.

"I'm not hungry," I murmured.

"We're all hurting, but neglecting yourself isn't going to do him or you any good, Ez. He would want you to take care of yourself."

"He's *dead*, J.T.," I snapped.

The same righteous anger I'd felt at my mother's death was starting to settle over me again. My cousin's death had been senseless. I had no proof and yet I also had no doubt the Order was behind it. If they couldn't take his magic, they would take him from me another way. Especially when I needed him the most. Yet, that tiny voice in the back of my head that sometimes sounded like him whispered "I saw it coming." His last words to me. Had he seen the shooter and purposely pushed me out of the way? Or was it something more? He'd acted strangely subdued after I'd met Aoife. Had he seen something in his dream?

"If you won't eat something for him, then do it for me," Avery said, appearing in the Council meeting room. I hadn't paid much attention to the somber and subdued black and greys she wore. Her eyes were red-rimmed, but she'd hidden it well with make-up. She looked far less perky than usual and I wasn't used to seeing her without her signature head-phones slung around her neck. She looked more grown up in mourning. She took one of the wraps J.T. offered and took a bite. If she could eat, I supposed I could do the same. I yanked the food out of J.T.'s hand and shoved it in my mouth, making a show of taking a big bite.

He held his hands up in surrender and left the room. Avery sat down beside me. "You have a right to be pissed off."

"Some Savior I am. I couldn't even stop a damn bullet."

"You're not a superhero, Ezri. Des never thought you were."

I let out a harsh bark of laughter. "Did you know he told me when we were younger that he was jealous of my destiny? Bet he's not jealous now."

"I don't blame you either. So don't sit here and act like this was your fault. You didn't pull the trig-ger," Avery said, her voice growing stronger, buoyed by her own emotions.

"He was with me. We got sloppy, thinking because I'd bound the other's magic that the Order couldn't touch us. I brought him along. So yeah, it is my fault. I'm so fucking tired of people dying, because of me. First my mother and now Desmond."

Avery tossed her partially eaten wrap on a nearby chair and grabbed both my wrists in her hands. 'You are not going to do that. You are not going to spiral like this, you hear me? You can grieve and be angry at the son-of a-bitch who did pull that trigger. But there was nowhere Desmond would have rather been than by your side. You remember that, okay?"

"How are you handling this so well? You just got married."

"Because I knew who I was marrying." She wiped fresh tears from her cheeks. "You need to use that anger and fire inside of you. Find who did this and bring them to justice. If you want to honor Desmond, you do that. You win the battle so that this, all of it means something."

I looked down at her hands wrapped around my wrists and pulled back so that I could lace my fingers between hers. "You have my word. I am going to get justice for Desmond. No matter what."

I let go of her hands and reached for the pendant at my throat. I hadn't been able to access his magic and I'd been trying. Hearing his voice one more time would make this so much easier. As I turned to study the sun in the sky overhead, the world settled around me as the balance between light and dark magic returned to equilibrium. There was a time that the balance would have filled me with a renewed sense of hope, but not now. Now it meant the eventual trudge toward winter and the rise of darkness. I had yet another destiny to fulfill, but the Order should be terrified of what's coming. They might think they've won, but they'd unleashed something I hadn't felt in a long while. A reckoning was coming and if I had my way, they weren't going to survive it.

QUICK AUTHOR'S NOTE

OH MAN, this book was probably the hardest of the series to write (and I know how the whole thing ends!). Since the very beginning on the series' creation, I knew that Desmond was going to die. And I even knew how it was going to happen. All these years later, that piece hasn't changed. And if you've read enough fantasy novels, you know that at some point, the hero is going to lose their mentor. Sure,

Desmond was more of a peer to Ezri but she did rely on him and he did guide her home.

I loved tracing their family roots back to Ireland and creating that sense that everyone spent so much time worrying about the first prophecy, they never really thought about what happened afterward. Oh, and her grandmother is just a hoot to write!

As always, thanks must be paid to my lovely beta readers and editor for helping me create the best story possible. And I know for a fact three of them cried at Desmond's passing.

If you're worried about whether Ezri might fall back into old habits, turn the page for your preview of the final book...

ABOUT THE AUTHOR

Sarah Biglow is a *USA Today* bestselling author. She lives in Massachusetts with her husband and son. She is a licensed attorney and spends her days combatting employment discrimination as an Investigator with the Massachusetts Commission Against Discrimination.

You can find an up-to-date list of all my books here